All The Leaving

—m—

Sometimes what you're left with is all you ever needed

Michelle Espinosa

ISBN: 0615945465
ISBN 13: 9780615945460

Dedicated to you. Find out what you do well and go out and do it for the world. The world needs you.

Acknowledgments

Without my mother who taught me tenacity, this book would never have come to be. If Eric had not insisted I write this book I might never have gone beyond the first chapter and Doriandra depositing me in a remote location to finish without distraction it would never have been completed. If it weren't for Bruce insisting recently that I locate myself, I might well have gone so far from this book I would never have come back. I'm grateful for them. By guiding me toward what you now hold in your hands, they gave me an invaluable gift.

There have been many generous friends who read my drafts of this or the adaptations, who were honest with me about my work like John, Richard, Gregg, Michael, Katie, Bonnie, and Ken who kept me striving to be a better writer.

All this would seem enough but it was the kindness and generosity of Sofia and Juan in Mexico City who saw something in me and took a chance to publish All the Leaving in Spanish that inspired me to see it through.

I must in utter humility and deepest gratitude offer thanks to my teacher, H. E. Garchen Rinpoche. Thank you, dear teacher, for inspiring me toward service of others rather than focus on myself.

Heartfelt thank you to Homeboy Industries in Los Angeles, California, where I continue to find strength and support and build belief in myself and to Rinchen Choling in Arcadia, California, for providing a home for Tibetan Buddhist teachings and retreats in the Drikung Kagyu lineage.

Tulsa calls herself a tourist and mostly she is a tourist of her own heart. She travels around it but has been unwilling to look into the far reaches where tragedy and heartbreak reside.

I knew I couldn't do what the character was doing and remain so far from the depths of my own heart. So, in the act of writing this book, I went in and set myself to look closely and pay attention to what I found.

I wrote this book over years toward the latter half of my fifteen year marriage. I was continuously traumatized by events and in that state of fragmentation and terrible imbalance, my only succor was to express all the unexpressed most shredded parts of my heart and soul.

For me it was about longing and alienation. It was about the need for human connection and how we can literally keep lifting ourselves up and carry on regardless of the damage and can even eventually heal.

For Tulsa and the other characters in the story it became more about family trauma and how we carry it on our backs and harbor its darkness in our hearts as though it were too precious to let go. We keep it with us to the point of letting it destroy any chance for our own happiness.

Feeling more connection and love for Mexico but not blessed with knowing my father's family has always weighed heavily on my heart. Mexico became that lover whose warmth and touch is indescribable but fleeting though we live together for many years.

My father had brown skin, dark hair, and green eyes. His chin was cleft like mine. He was bilingual. He was a technical writer. His mother spoke only Spanish and his father was deceased by the time I was born. He had two sisters. I have nothing of my birth family beyond this. So here is a story from others, from everyone I have known and loved. I listened and paid attention not only to my own heart but also to theirs.

This book is the ballad that I heard.

Michelle Espinosa

Los Angeles, October 2013

I was tricked by memory into believing that life is a river of sorrows. Now I know, after committing memory to page, that it doesn't occupy our minds so much as our hearts. It's less about what happened, or if it happened at all, than it is about what our hearts can endure. Putting memory to paper unburdened my heart and delivered me to my own true life. I am now free.

I offer you this faulty account of my family: My mother who left me when I was five years-old; my abuela (grandmother) and spirit guardian; and my grandfather, Pops, who raised me until I shot him and he stopped speaking to me.

Here's what I know now: sometimes what you're left with is all you ever needed.

–Tulsa

1

Three sounds have stayed with me: startling, reality-popping pistol fire, the loud crackle and crunch of ripened walnuts when you walk on them, and the sound of my mother singing.

The pistol had been part of the dowry from Señor Ramos, my grandfather's father-in-law, to Pops, my grandfather. It was handed to him on his wedding day, the day he married his sixteen year-old bride, Concepción, my grandmother, my abuela, my spirit guardian. At the sound of that pistol firing, my body recoiled as if the bullet were tearing through me. I remember the silence of time that had frozen for a moment after.

I can see the black walnuts carpeting the yard I often went to during the bright white summer of my ninth year. And my mother singing, the only sound of her I was able to keep with me, a melancholy lullaby.

When I was a girl and had not yet collected any memories, the world and the universe were infinite mysteries to me. I was unaware then of what all the leaving and being left behind would feel like. Since then, when anyone left me or I left anyone else, my world became a smaller place of lessening significance. I heard that when you are older you know yourself more, that you understand the world better. I only understood what those around me and the small world we occupied had made of me and took out of me.

The only lasting significance in life for me began one cold autumn night when I was five years old. I was abandoned by my mother and had been tucked in the unfamiliar bed of my grandfather who I did not know. He slept on the sofa and left me to sleep alone in a small bedroom.

I was shaken from a raucous and bone rattling thunderstorm pounding the window of the second story apartment. And just when I thought I might shatter into a million pieces, an apparition appeared next to the bed. It was my grandmother at sixteen, wearing her quinceañera dress. She was immediately comforting as she blazed in a bloom of spiking light and ever so sweetly smiled down at me and winked. I knew at that moment that my mother had been right when she told me that my abuela was my guardian angel. My mother's last words to me were "You never have to feel alone or be afraid."

Not a single day passed after that visitation that I did not feel looked after, or at least accompanied. I was convinced she was with me but after that night she didn't appear to me again until twenty years later.

By then I lived in a cottage with Lance on the edge of a metropolis. Joy overtook me at the sight of her. Then I noticed that she was weeping and the sorrow in her eyes spoke of separation and tragedy.

I felt a vicious pain in my chest, a terrible longing and grief. Before I could understand what it meant, she faded from me. I looked around the room in a panicky desperate search for her, for a sense of her presence. I was in that moment terribly lost to life, to the world around me. I had no sense of belonging, something that had been tenuous yet thankfully existed because of my abuela, my Concepción, my guardian.

The Mexican blanket I have had since childhood looked and smelled like it belonged to someone else. The cottage I lived in was suddenly wrong like all the rooms had been lifted, shuffled and dropped on me. I wandered through its tiny rooms, searching for any familiarity. Everything occupying its spaces was as flat and distant as a picture briefly glimpsed in a magazine.

I had felt an edgy sense of damage lingering at the back of my neck for two weeks prior to that night; the muscle's steel sinews piled into a widow's hump. There was a weight against me as if my entire life had rushed up and piled whole at my back. I clearly had to put a stop to it. A more severely humped-back was about to overtake me. I could think of no other solution than to secretly use my boyfriend's old manual typewriter and hurriedly record and hopefully cast out a seemingly inexorable past. When I was alone, I began to write in a corner of the tiny cottage.

The cottage was one of five in an overgrown courtyard. Juniper trees towered over the small building and darkened it within though it was summer. Sheets of cobwebs hung on the trees and on inside corners. Dust had long settled indoors and out. Though the sun was white-hot, as was common in the area that time of year, the tiny house was dark and cold.

I had known myself up to that point as Tulsa, named after the town where I was born, a name Pops stuck me with. I never knew my family but I still had a faint sense of who I was held together by my connection to that lovely though invisible spirit who was with me for so long.

I had to beat the words out on that old typewriter because the ribbon was so dry. Still the "I" would not imprint itself onto the page. I wrote of my earliest memory:

A v ew through the w ndow of my mother's Volkswagen Beetle, of m les and m les of dusty, desolate land strewn w th power l nes and o l f elds.

I wrote about how fear felt the first time in that car, how striking, how palpable it was in the lengthening distance between my mother and me as we drove down the street toward the apartment building where we would part.

I remembered the first sight of my grandfather, not much taller than I was at five years old. He was under five feet in height with a thick white braid down his back, Van Dyke beard and a furrowed brow at the sight of me. We were to become something of a family, my grandfather and me. Both of us were left behind by all others. I was to call him "Pops" but he refused to call me by my given name, Concepción. It was the name of his long since deceased wife. She was Concepción, I was not.

The unrelenting memories of my past all came drumming out onto pages I kept hidden under the cushion of a chair in the front room of the cottage. But it relieved none of the unspecified anxiety.

When the night came that my grandmother's spirit left me, my soul and my body must have known what was about to happen considering the hump growing across the back of my shoulders, and the immediacy, almost urgency of the memories of her. None of that mattered. My heart refused to believe it. I cried all night until after there were no tears left.

In the morning, I dragged myself, sloshing through the tear-flooded floor of the cottage, to the short narrow kitchen to put on the tea kettle. Through the dusty, dark, screen-covered window, I caught sight of Lance outside prominently displaying that big-toothed winning smile of his. He was chatting with the neighbor. He had been out collecting rent for the landlady who lived in the large front house all alone, hidden away, seeing only Lance (her lackey) and delivery boys.

The next door neighbor laughed, her teeth straight and bright, eyes flashing in a bit of sun shining down on only the two of them. The kettle whistled, drawing their attention, so I ducked out of sight. I made tea and sat with it in the chair stuffed with my hidden stack of typed memories. I heard Lance pass by outside the cottage and thought he might be headed back in to be with me but instead he went to the back door of the landlady's house and slipped inside as he had been doing for too long by then. As I had since the first time, I wished it to be the day when Lance would refuse the life he was choosing and return to me. I thought, let this be the day I do not feel so bereft.

Naturally there was more to it than that. I'm the Mexico of my grandmother, the love sickness of my mother, the outlandishness and artistry of my grandfather and the no-name nomadism of my father. But I could not see it then. When my spirit guardian departed she took my sight with her. I no longer saw into things. I had no more intuitive guidance. I lost all sense of nuance. I looked at my life and only saw all the leaving.

Maybe because my story is linked to hers, to my abuela Concepción, my namesake. Though I only know what I learned from my grandfather, Pops, and Rose, my mother, and what I figured out by what was not being said. I don't know much about her life before she was sixteen, before that terrible night in the desert, in Mexico.

2

In the northern Mexican desert, 1931, under a mean white sun, my abuela Concepción, sixteen, looked on while her step-father, Señor Ramos gave his sixteen year-old son a Colt .45 Six Shooter. He then kissed his very pregnant wife goodbye and climbed onto the back of a truck to ride away with a few rancheros heading back into town.

"I'm going to be right back," he told them before the truck drove off down the highway.

Concepción's mother put her arm around Concepción's shoulders and took her back to the red delivery truck. The hood was up and engine steaming and all the doors were opened to keep it cooler inside. The back of the truck was full of unpainted, hand-carved masks of crow, skull, wolf, lamb, and devil, all stacked around their luggage. Blankets were laid out for Concepción's mother to rest on. Concepción helped her in and tried to cool her with a handmade fan from

Veracruz. Armando went to the front and was soon deep asleep from the heat. Concepción's mother searched through a cowhide satchel and took out a monedero (a coin purse) and gave it to Concepción.

"Your grandmother gave those escudos to me and now I want you to have them," she told her daughter.

Concepción opened the bag and removed a hand full of gold coins, some wrapped, some not.

"Be very careful with those. Don't even let the wind touch them."

Concepción put the coins back into the satchel. Her mother took out Concepción's quinceañera photo for them both to admire.

"What a beautiful quinceañera. I can see you in your wedding dress. The most beautiful bride in town."

Concepción put the satchel down next to her mother to use as a pillow. She laid down in her mother's arm and sighed from a heavy heart.

"We don't know them," Concepción said.

"Try to be nice to them, my darling. Remember, they're your family now too. Here, let me kiss you."

Concepción moved so that her mother could easily kiss her forehead.

Later, in the middle of the night, outside, Armando stood back in the desert staring at the truck. Agonized screams came from inside.

In the truck, Concepción had looked away during the worst screams and, when she looked back down, she saw that the umbilical cord was wrapped around the infant's throat. She removed the cord and pulled him free of the birth canal. She put the tiny body in her mother's arm and lay down next to her. Concepción felt a tugging at her soul while her mother cradled her in one arm and her son's cold body in the other and sang a lullaby as she lay dying.

As soon as he heard that lullaby, all the tension went out of Armando's body and he went back into the cab to sleep.

When her Mother stopped singing, Concepción put her fingers over her mother's lips to feel for her breath. She put her ear against her mother's chest to listen for her heart beat and passed out to sleep from exhaustion with her cheek against her mother's cold breast.

At first light of morning, Concepción removed herself from the icy pair and put a blanket over them. She went out with the satchel and saw that Armando was still asleep in the cab of the truck. She took the Colt which he had left on the dash and walked into the desert a little.

She removed the wedding photo with Señor Ramos and her step-brother from the satchel and propped it against a cactus. She backed up and carelessly aimed and fired. That Colt was not only a very large pistol, it had a kick that could knock a man down. She missed and landed on her butt. The shot startled Armando awake. He saw Concepción with the pistol and, having determined that she wasn't a threat to him, Armando went to look in the back of the truck.

A blanket covered the bodies but blood could still be seen here and there. Just as Concepción was cocking the pistol to try again, she heard a vehicle. She and Armando looked up and watched the ranchero's truck that took Señor Ramos away coming back up the highway toward them.

Later she cried molten tears over the graves of her mother and brother. She didn't know her new family and now she remained with them to continue north to a world of white faces. She kept hearing her mother; try to be nice to them, my darling, they are your family.

One bright hot and dusty day, the street where she lived with her father and brother was unusually empty of the families who had been spending summer outside, children playing, adults chatting, grilling, and waiting for it to be cool enough to go indoors. The stillness was pronounced given the absence of the usual tension in the neighborhood. Everyone either knew or was related to someone who had been picked up by immigration. On that day, all the families had trekked to a nearby park where they could hopefully enjoy the afternoon and forget La Migra.

Hundreds of families had gathered in the park. Concepción's step-father, Señor Ramos, and step-brother, Armando, had gone there to solicit the crowd. They weaved their way through the park holding up long poles that displayed the masks they brought from Mexico. The animal faces were painted with vibrant colors and drew a lot of attention.

Families grilled and children played while mothers looked on and gossiped.

Nearby, armed officers readied themselves paramilitary style for a sweep of the park. Paddy-wagons and buses were lined up, trains heading to Mexico waited.

Concepción had stayed behind in the two room structure they lived in to continue her work. The wedding photo she had tried shooting was intact and on the wall by the door. The building was one of many low cost one and two room houses lining a dirt road in view of city hall.

Concepción's father had arranged for an elderly neighbor to watch over her. The sturdy eighty year-old woman sat outside on a bench in the shade of a Bougainvillea against the next building. She smoked hand rolled cigarettes in silence while Concepción worked. Concepción had earlier thrown open the door and all the windows in an attempt to circulate the stifling air. It provided scant relief. The air had been still all day. Concepción had been sitting as straight as a dancer at the worktable facing the window overlooking the street. Her hair, pulled back into a shiny, dark brown braid, reached past the seat of the stool.

A car drove by and Concepción hurried to slam the window against the billowing dust kicked up from the dirt road. She caught glimpse of the driver briefly and wondered what a gringo was doing there. She inspected the lamb mask she had almost finished and saw that a layer of grainy dirt from the street had attached itself to the tacky surface. She cursed and tossed the mask on the floor.

The car made a U-turn at the end of the block and tried another pass. Then it parked at the end of the street and the driver walked back down. The man stopped to speak to the neighbor woman. Concepción could see them through the open door. She randomly selected another mask to paint so she could be occupied while eavesdropping.

"Buenos dias, Señora" The man said.

"Buenos dias, Señor. Can I help you?" the woman asked.

"Thank you, yes. I'm looking for Señor Ramos."

Hearing her father's name, Concepción impulsively put on the nearest mask, a crow. She looked down and, realizing it was a skull she had selected to paint, she shivered.

"This is his house, Señor," the neighbor said, "But he is not at home."

"Muchas gracias," the man said, "I will leave a message for him."

Concepción glanced back. The man was using the side of the house as a surface to write a note. As he did so, he looked inside. She felt a strange yet familiar tugging at her arms and turned away.

"Señorita," the woman called to Concepción.

"Yes?" Concepción responded without turning back.

"This man is asking for Señor Ramos," the woman told Concepción.

"Yes, I know Señora but at the moment I am occupied," Concepción responded. "Tell him to please leave," she said loud enough for him to hear.

"Excuse me, Señorita," the man said to Concepción's back. "Please excuse me for interrupting you."

Concepción turned and looked at him through the crow mask. Pops, in the doorway, hat in hand, seemed boyish though he was around thirty and handsome in a rugged sort of way despite his small stature. She was struck with a sudden déjà vu as if she had seen him in some other time, another world. She turned back around and started painting the black eyes of the skull.

"My father is not home, Señor. I can tell him you were here," she said through the crow mask and with her back to him, fighting the pull of his presence there. Pops stepped in saying "I did not hear you," prompting the woman outside to show him her machete so he stepped back. "Thank you, tell him a friend—" he began. Two gunshots rang out. Concepción looked at the Señora.

There was chaos in the park. Families were running, tripping over abandoned picnics. A city issue boot came down on a lamb mask, cracking it in half. Hundreds of people ran out of the park. Armed officers advanced on them. Mothers ran with children.

The poles of masks were knocked over and Señor Ramos fell. Armando rushed back to help him as officers advanced on them and one hit Señor Ramos across the head with a baton, knocking him off his feet again. Armando helped his father and knocked the officer down, gaining needed time for them to get into the crowd running away.

Once they cleared the park and any immediate danger, Armando sat Señor Ramos down behind a building and took off his shirt to have his father press against his head wound before continuing.

Outside Señor Ramos's house, a man rushed up to tell them, "La Migra is in the park! They are armed!"

Concepción threw her mask off and pushed past the stranger to run out to the street. "Who did they get?" Concepción implored. The man glanced at the stranger who had remained by the house with his hat and the note in his hands.

"You and the Señora go back inside," the man told Concepción, looking suspiciously at the stranger. "I will pass again to check on you." He addressed the stranger contemptuously. "Is there anything I can help you with, Señor?"

Ignoring him, the stranger followed after Concepción who had run to the neighbor and was escorting her into the house.

"Excuse me, Señorita?"

More men came from down the street. The man Concepción had been talking to was swept up in the crowd running through the street, knocking on doors and windows.

There was more gunfire in the distance.

The last of the mayhem swept past leaving an even more pronounced stillness behind.

After taking the neighbor inside, Concepción sat her at the table and closed the door and windows. Before closing the last window she looked out into the street.

The stranger's car was still parked a few houses away but there was no sign of him. Concepción offered water to the neighbor and sat at the table with her. There was a knock at the door. Concepción opened the door and faced the stranger. He handed her the note.

"Goodbye, Señor," she said, snatching the note and crossing her arms. "I will give my father your message."

"I cannot in good conscience leave you and this lady here alone under these circumstances– "

"Señor," Concepción began firmly, cutting him off.

In that moment she saw Armando helping Señor Ramos up the street toward her.

"His leg is broken."

Pops rushed into the street to assist Armando. Concepción rushed to help Armando with her father so that Pops would not be able to. She didn't want this unfamiliar gringo looking after him. She and Armando brought him into the house and sat him at the table. Pops waited outside.

"Seat our friend, what's wrong with you?" Señor Ramos snapped at Concepción.

She moved a chair out from the table and gestured for Pops to have it.

"Welcome! Come in my friend, come in," Señor Ramos managed to shout out to Pops though he was in pain. "The mescal," he told Concepción. "Sit down," he told his son.

"We were fortunate this time," Señor Ramos said, raising his cup. "Salute."

Pops raised his cup. "To more good fortune."

Concepción gathered from their conversation that Pops had previously worked with her father and had come to tell him about a stone-laying job.

Armando was sent out to find someone to look after his father's injuries. A few neighbor's came and all determined his ankle was sprained and he would have to stay off it as much as possible. An ad-hock brace was constructed and someone else brought a crutch.

A few lights were on around her street. People gathered in small groups here and there outside, talking in hushed tones. Concepción served the men tequila and sat at the worktable. She watched them talk and resented their relaxed manner. Her father addressed the stranger familiarly and treated him like an old family friend.

3

One day Pops told Señor Ramos that he wanted to paint Concepción's portrait and would pay for her time. She would not agree to stop painting the masks.

"I'm not going to stop working so this stranger can examine me with his eyes." But she did not object to him painting while she worked. It was money for the house and now that her father was mending a sprained ankle, how could she refuse?

The painting itself possessed a mystical quality. The room around her was filled with animal faces, some raw, some painted, all facing forward except Concepción. She is turned away and concentrated on finer than usual detail.

When she wasn't working on the masks, she tended to her father and brother. She and Pops never exchanged a word outside of courtesies and formalities. Pops and Señor Ramos, on the other hand, found many opportunities to converse in hushed tones. They would change the subject or stop all together whenever Concepción was nearby. They often smoked outside after dinner and she would hear her name or notice their glances at her.

Soon Armando joined them. They laughed together and Señor Ramos would pat Armando's back. The door would be open and Concepción watched them out of the corner of her eye while she cleaned up after their meal, swept, painted.

She felt conspired against. It struck her in the heart and made her weep when she was alone. A terrible sense of separation from them began in those days. Every tear that fell from her eyes took with it a bit of her family that had lived in her. She missed the bright light of her mother most then.

Pops liked to think that he was not only painting Concepción's portrait for the first time but was, as Pops would recount it later, capturing her soul. That must have been why she would only give him her back. She had lost too much of herself already. He painted with an intensity not lost on any of them in that house but the distractions of their new routine held most of their attention.

Since Señor Ramos could not walk yet, he had to rely on Armando to work twice as hard. In addition to selling masks, Armando performed menial labor for contractors who knew Señor Ramos and Pops. Armando had to be out from dawn until late night. Which meant

Concepción was spared little sleep in making sure her step-brother ate hot meals and his clothes were clean and ready. She never complained but she was often so tired, she would weep at night, wishing her mother were there to take care of her.

Whenever Armando caught her weeping, he would slap her head or pinch her. They had to share a bed because the space in the room would allow nothing else. Just because she couldn't sleep, she reasoned, why shouldn't they sleep if they can? She had no right to wake anyone with her crying.

She still believed they had only her best interest at heart. But she also felt that by letting that gringo spend so much time at their house, they were going too far. She didn't want that man there all the time. She had work to do. She had to look after an injured father, working brother, the household, and help the family business by painting masks and keeping records.

It was too much to ask her to entertain the gringo every day. She didn't care how much money they were making for it. He paid only to paint her. Nobody said he was paying to stick around and drink with her father and brother. She looked forward to the day he finished his painting and left forever.

She tried not to look him in the eye or look at him at all, even while moving by him in the cramped quarters of their house. Whenever she came near him, his face would light up and he would jump out of the way or always maneuver to help her, carrying this and lifting that. She wanted to tell him she had been doing fine without him. She might have said something except for the sexual energy she felt between them. That attraction kept her quiet and generally annoyed and confused.

Then the day came when Pops was to bring the finished painting for an informal unveiling. Concepción woke in very good spirits. She got up early so she could clean the house in every corner. She cooked all day. She was especially affectionate with her father and brother. Señor Ramos enjoyed the attention, it irritated Armando and he kept pushing her away. But she didn't let his moodiness bother her. It meant nothing because the gringo was leaving.

She even treated Pops better when he arrived with the chamois-covered portrait. She addressed herself directly to him, smiled, and tried to engage him in conversation after offering him a seat.

"It must seem strange after you finish a painting, Señor Burns. Mescal?" She asked, holding the bottle and a cup.

Pops beamed and nodded. "Strange, Señorita?" he asked while she poured his drink.

"You know, the end of your work. Fortunately you have a painting to show for it. All we have is the return to a normal life."

"Concepción!" Señor Ramos barked.

Armando flashed a deadly poisonous glance at her.

"Señor Ramos," Pops said, standing. "Before I take advantage of your hospitality, I must say what I came here to say."

Concepción, still happy, was curious what speech this man so full of himself had prepared to impress them. She handed out cups, poured the mescal and waited to hear.

"Señor, with your blessing, I would like to ask for the hand of your daughter in marriage."

The bottle of mescal fell from her and broke apart against the floor. Both Señor Ramos and Armando jumped to their feet. Armando looked at his father, attempting to gauge the situation according to his father's reaction. It took a moment for Concepción to register the accident and move to clean it. She knelt down to clean it up. Pops leapt up to help her pick the shards off the floor.

"Right now I can assure a roof over our heads, food, and in a few years, God willing, children," he told her, looking up at her. "You will have education and medical care. I will keep you safe and you will never have to do anything you don't want to."

She gave her stepfather an incredulous look on her way to throw away the broken bottle but he shot her a glance that effectively kept her quiet and seething "Will you marry me, Concepción?" Pops asked her.

"Pops, any good young woman would be honored and fortunate to have you as a husband," her father said.

Concepción searched their faces while none of them had the nerve to look her in the eye. She was furious. Armando discreetly twisted the flesh at her side, to stop her from crying. He made her serve them soup and tortillas. She clanked and splashed through serving and refilling their tequila until, finally, she could stand it no longer.

"Señor," she said to Pops, "Don't think you can treat me like a ranch animal that can be traded from one man to the other."

Armando slapped her. She slapped him back and ran outside.

—◆◆—

I heard the story the first time from Pops when I was eight years old and later from my mother. When he proclaimed his love and devotion to Concepción, I cut him off.

"She was a kid. You can come down out of the clouds."

"Tulsa, your grandmother and I loved each other. I invested in Señor Ramos's modest business, helped it grow, made money to keep Concepción's family well looked after."

Señor Ramos had wanted to move to New Mexico and get Armando involved in vocational education. He wanted to marry his step-daughter to a citizen so that Armando could get his papers. He also had plans to start a masonry business and was looking for a partner.

"Where are they now?" I asked.

"New Mexico," he said.

"How come you never talk to them or get Christmas cards from them?"

"Because we're not that sort of a family," Pops had told me.

"How can you say she loved you, when you had to buy her?"

"I didn't buy her. To begin with, we came to respect and appreciate each other's company when I painted her portrait for the first time."

—〰—

Pops came outside looking for Concepción and discovered her in front of the house gazing at the stars. He stood near her and looked up.

"Did you ever see the sky filled with mostly stars from horizon to horizon?" Concepción asked Pops.

He shook his head. He was dumbfounded by her natural grace and beauty. Her hands were full of dirt. Dirt was caked under her fingernails. She held a dirt covered coin purse in her hand.

"I did. In the desert, in Mexico. I looked up at the stars and remembered how long the light takes to come here. They are already gone by the time we see them," she said, pointing. "They do not exist after their journey to our eyes. The sky is full of lies. Only the moon is true." She looked at Pops. "I know my father thinks he has no choice than to send me away with you, Señor, but they need me to take care of them now that my mother is gone."

"Ever since I met you, I have not slept."

Concepción wondered how much sleep she might have had if she had never met him.

"You would have me believe you have not slept for weeks?"

"If you marry me, I will pay for your father and brother to relocate and start a business."

"You are exaggerating."

"You are my muse."

"You are drunk."

"Whether or not you agree to marry me, Señorita, I will spend the rest of my life trying to capture your beauty in my paintings," Pops declared.

He never said a truer thing before or since.

"Señor, forgive me, but how can I be sure what you say is true about my father's business? Will you sign your name to it?"

Pops was knocked out by her, stunned. She was "sharp as a tack" as he'd say. Pops married Concepción before she turned seventeen, and, to demonstrate his faith and trust in her he added her name to everything and let her take care of all the business and household affairs. He kept his contractual agreement and helped her father and brother relocate to New Mexico to carry out their plans, leaving Concepción with Pops who they knew was at least in love with her and hopefully never cruel.

Pops was a mason by trade and an artist at night. His subjects were always female nudes. Painting after painting of naked women he either knew or solicited for in art photography magazines. Night after night he affirmed the beauty of women's bodies and lived by day denying Concepción's soul, or so it felt to her when she watched the strange women coming and going and hardly spent any time at all with Pops. But she considered herself modern and accepted that she was now living the life of an artist's wife.

She was relieved that they slept in separate beds for now. Pops was in the studio and she now had the bedroom. She went to bed every night with her virginity intact. But her mind wandered through the closed doors and into the studio where a strange woman was lying naked for Pops' gaze. She thought about his eyes studying her every slope and curve, the weight of her breasts, the cleft of her sex.

Concepción was by then seventeen years old. She wasn't painting masks anymore. She wasn't enjoying the literature and art she had been accustomed to in Mexico. Now her time was taken up with taking care of all the household cooking, cleaning, banking, his art bookkeeping; his secretary, maid, assistant.

"Señor, I am grateful that you have helped my father and brother but I am not the housemaid. I am your wife, not your free labor. I was not put on this earth to work for you."

"Where does a girl your age come up with such ideas?" Pops asked, truly bewitched.

"Señor, do you think there are no books or conversations in Mexico?"

"Are you making fun of me?" Pops asked, disconcerted and unusually uncertain of himself. "Now, Concepción, let's not say anything we'll regret later."

"Why not if it's how my heart feels right now? Maybe they could prevent me from speaking my mind at my step-father's house but this is my house as well as yours and I intend to speak my mind here."

"Good god, girl, wherever did you learn to speak English?"

"Señor, we have schools in Mexico."

"Why did your mother leave, if I may ask?"

"You may but it will do you no good," she said. "No one is willing to speak of it. Not even to me."

They sat at the table together sipping their tea. Concepción tried not to show that she was aware of Pops studying her.

"Señora Burns?" Pops stood and offered his hand. "Will you allow me the insolence of believing I can capture your exceptional beauty in another painting?"

Concepción stood and gave him her hand. Pops led her into his studio. Until then, she had not yet been alone with Pops in his studio. It was difficult to keep her mind off imagining a naked woman in there.

Pops unveiled a few paintings of the women. Concepción was drawn closer to study his technique and brush style. She was fascinated by the sensuality of the paintings, something that was not remotely apparent in the women Pops introduced her to before disappearing with them into his bedroom studio.

"Tell me," she asked, admiring the work, "Why do you do this? Do these women take their clothes off only for money? Are they professionals or desperate? What is it you are doing here?"

"There are few things in nature that express the purity and beauty of creation. To me as a man, the female body is the closest to a true expression of beauty."

"Is that what you say so the women take off their clothes?"

"Not my wife. If a man is virile, his wife will want him," Pops explained. "A man who comes to a woman and takes from her what she might have freely given him knows no pleasure beyond what he steals from life. A man who lets a woman give herself to him allows life to bless him with its finest joys and pleasures."

"You are used to women saying yes to you," Concepción noted matter-of-factly.

"What woman would refuse adoration?"

Concepción nodded with a little smile. "I think it is true," she admitted.

"You would make me the happiest man on the face of the earth."

Pops had put a straight-backed chair in the middle of the room and directed a light on it. Concepción sat down. Pops poured her a glass of water from a decanter and put it on the floor near her.

"In case you are thirsty. Are you comfortable?"

Concepción nodded, feeling fine in the chair but tight in her stomach.

"I'd like to sketch you first. Would that be all right?"

She was enjoying the respectful formality. It reminded her of family dinners on special occasions. A languorous air descended on the room. Into the night she sat there watching Pops study her, the strokes of his pencil, his penetrating focus. Concepción realized, after watching him in silence for hours, that Pops was looking for something rather than looking at something.

Pops swung away one sketch and began another, continuing his intensive search. After the tenth sketch Concepción noticed he had only been sketching her face. She looked down at herself, clothed and somewhat formal in that chair. Then she looked around at Pops' other subjects, all nudes. They smiled and winked at her or so it seemed to Concepción who in that moment started to truly fall in love with Pops. She sensed Pops was in new territory sketching a clothed woman but she said nothing.

She sat for him every night after for weeks. Because there were no models coming over and Pops was between jobs, he was with her at breakfast and for dinner every night. He pulled out her chair and stood when she entered or left the room. He had always been adoring but she had not spent so much time with him.

Concepción spent sleepless nights alone in her room, her attention always on Pops lying alone in his studio on the rollaway. Often she believed Pops was thinking about her at the same time and that she could feel when his thoughts were on her and her heart would quicken almost painfully.

In the morning when she would pass him to and from the bathroom, still in her nightgown, Pops in his robe, she no longer averted her eyes. She looked at him and smiled, lighting the two of them up. She looked more closely when he was in his undershirt, examining his thick, muscular upper arms, the tuft of hair on his chest disappearing under his shirt. She began to enjoy the masculinity she had been avoiding.

One night after they both went into their rooms and shut their doors, Concepción took off her clothes and stood naked before her mirror and wondered how Pops would see her and became very excited at the thought.

To take a break from painting, Pops took Concepción to an exhibit of Impressionist art at the county museum. It did not hold her interest. "There is more to existence than the play of light on the world," she commented then pulled him into a nearby exhibition of primitive art.

"But we may not find it in the past," Pops told her.

"Or the future," she said.

"And where is that, our future?"

"You and me?"

"Yes."

"Together. Where else?"

Pops almost choked up. He looked at Concepción with naked adoration like he had just discovered how precious a gem had been in his hands. Concepción put her arm through his and squeezed it affectionately as she would many times in their years together.

"Don't worry, pendejo, I'm not going anywhere," she told him.

When Pops finished his painting of her and wanted her to finally see it, she encouraged him to unveil it ceremoniously as he did the first time in her father's house. Pops opened a bottle of schnapps and, after pouring two glasses, he handed her one and raised his.

"To my muse," he toasted and swung away the chamois, revealing the painting.

Concepción hid her disappointment under a smile. Pops stepped back beside her to gaze at the painting along with her, shoulder to shoulder. All the sensuousness of his nudes was missing. It was skillful but lacked soul as though her clothes and reserve had obscured the flame of life within her from his view. She took it down from the easel and set it aside. She held up her hand to stop his protestations.

Concepción picked up a fresh canvas and put it on the easel. Then she stepped over to the chair and removed her clothes before sitting down. Pops couldn't help staring at the perfection of her beauty. She blushed and looked away. Pops gently raised her chin to see into her eyes. He sketched quickly, darting his gaze back and forth between her and his image of her. She giggled self-consciously. Pops offered her wine and she sipped it. He sketched her roguish smile, the wine glass in her hand resting on her upper leg, and the blush in her cheeks.

He sketched at feverish pace, sending chills down her spine. Concepción took sips of her wine and squirmed in the seat, impressed by the entirely new and quite intense tickling between her legs. She felt a tugging at her soul, a terrible longing to be embraced by Pops. She held out her arms toward him. He put down his sketch and went to her.

They conceived my mother that night and baptized her Rosa-Marie after Concepción's mother. Pops called her Rose. He said, "She is perfection like the rose." It wasn't long before he had her in a bed of rose petals and attempted to paint her portrait. This proved difficult because she couldn't hold a pose and was only quiet while asleep. But he couldn't work without seeing her eyes.

For Pops the eyes were essential. He learned his lesson from that first painting of Concepción with her back to him. Pops tried to nudge Rose when she dosed off. It made her jolt awake and cry and brought Concepción in to scoop her up and whisk her away. Alone quite often, he longed to paint and grew restless. Concepción nursed Rose and to Pops they occupied a world together he was not equipped to enter.

Pops had so thoroughly convinced himself of his isolation from Concepción and Rose that even while in their company he was hardly there with them. He would watch them, smiled when they smiled, or laughed and nodded or shook his head to answer them, all the while his mind drifted in a fog. Concepción became aware of the distance in Pops' gaze. That distance was an icy invasion in her heart and it frightened her.

"You have to get formula from the market," Concepción told Pops one day.

"How can that be?"

"All of your brooding has soured my milk," she told him with pleading eyes and a harsh tone. "Why did you stop painting?" she asked him while washing out yet another baby bottle.

"The models won't relax when there is a crying baby."

"Then paint me, come on." Concepción took off clothes her on her way to the studio. As soon as she was naked in the chair and Pops was sketching, she relaxed enough for Rose to nurse again.

As Rose grew, Concepción would plead with Pops to spend more time with her. After he had finished one painting and was looking for his next model he took them on family excursions. Far above the laughing crowd and havoc of fairs and amusement parks, my mother would look to Pops to share with him the joy of the ride. But she always found him far away. In my mother's most exalted moments with Pops, he was as animated and spiritless as a marionette.

For Pops it was necessary to paint. When he did not paint he was disconnected from everything in the world. Painting was the precise fit for him, the exact place in which he was what he was born to be. When he didn't paint his soul was aimless and wanting. He had no idea how else to be in the world.

Rose was sixteen when it happened. A burst aneurysm and Concepción was gone.

4

One day when I was eight, I came home angry because a teacher had embarrassed me in front of
the class when I faltered while reading out loud. I had
talked back to her and was kept after school. I entered the
empty front room and dropped my pack and skateboard
on the sofa. I noticed Pops' keys on the table where he
usually left them. I wanted to tell him about what happened but his door was closed which meant he was with
a model. Half the time when he painted he was with a
model and the rest of the time he was alone finishing up
and would leave the door ajar.

For a couple of weeks while he painted with a model
I never saw him. He was in his room right after he came
home from work until long after I had gone to bed. He
wasn't around in the morning when I got up and ate cold
cereal alone.

On this particular day, when I was burning to com-
plain about how I had been teased at school and told I was

a retard, Pops' closed door was more of an affront than it had ever been. I tentatively knocked, almost regretting it as soon as I did it. I heard rustling and muffled voices and wondered if I ran into my room and shut the door whether Pops would think he had been hearing things. The door opened and Pops stepped out and closed it behind him.

"What happened? Is it a fire? Better be a natural disaster," he barked at me.

"I just…"

"Out with it, girl, I'm working."

"Never mind," I said and stomped into my room. "You don't care anyway!" I shouted loud enough for the naked woman in his room to hear me before closing the door in his face. I sat on my bed and waited for him to come in to reprimand me. After a while I opened my door a crack and peeked out. His door was closed. I leaned out to look into the apartment. It was empty. I tip-toed over to Pops' door and listened to the muffled voice of the model. Pops said something and she giggled. Then Pops chuckled.

I tried to imagine what his face looked like when he was laughing. His eyes generally sparkled and his mouth curved up at the edges but he never laughed around me. He only barked at me, though he had that look in his eyes like he was hiding a smile. I went back into my room and closed my door. I sat on my bed and looked out my window at the exposed fuselage in the aircraft graveyard next door. I picked out oddly mix-matched parts of a whole plane and imagined them together. I heard a jet and looked up in time to see the vapor trail across the sky and the plane disappearing from view. I imagined sitting with my mother on that plane. I'm pointing out the window at the aerial view of Pops' apartment building and we are laughing together.

When I told Pops my mother sang to me the night she left me with him, he denied it until later when he discovered his most precious painting was missing. It was the portrait of Concepción with Rose in her arms. Pops claimed that "the reason Rose came back in the first place was to steal my painting. You probably woke up and she had to rock you back to sleep before she could make her get-away."

"You're wrong, old man," I insisted every time he said it. "She came back for me. She came back to see me."

In an attempt to besmirch my mother's name and challenge my conviction, Pops told me about the thirty year-old biker who had shown up at the building to visit neighbors the year before I was born. He said, "Once Rose and that dude met, I couldn't keep her from him."

Not long after that dude came to the building, Rose bumped into him at the dumpster in back when she went out with the trash. From then on "a powerful force drew them together, stronger than the chains I used to keep them apart," Pops told me. "The force of That Dude (Pops' name for my father) wanting for himself a seventeen year-old virgin. The bastard," Pops said.

I rolled my eyes. Concepción was seventeen when he conceived Rose with her.

This was in 1962, mind you. Rose, in her platforms and strut, came out to the dumpster in back of the Arms Apartments, behind the carports. She tossed out the trash and nearly bumped into That Dude. He was out there drinking a beer and smoking a joint.

"Hey, wait a sec, don't be in such a hurry, beautiful. I think I just fell in love with you," he told her, putting out the joint.

Rose giggled. They were under a harsh, unflattering parking lot light. Though Rose was a natural beauty, the light had her makeup garish, almost clownish.

"Oh brother."

You like that? "Here, let me have a look at you, momma," he said, taking her hand. "Where are you hurrying off to? Some place good, I hope."

"Maybe."

"What's your name?"

"Rosa."

He took her by the waist to dance. "Rosa, like the rose? Why, I do believe your name suits you, Rose."

Rose giggled and That Dude swung her around like his own little dancing puppet until he had her laughing.

"I don't think I can let you go."

"That's what you say to all the girls you kidnap."

"Practically. You see right through me, though, don't you, Rose? There's something about you, can't keep my hands off of you."

"Then you toss me aside."

"I can't think of anything beyond you in my arms. After that, I could die. It's meant to be, Rose, I can feel it. I'm heading out tonight. You could come with me, sweet thing. I have to say, you are the prettiest girl outside of a magazine I have ever seen."

Rose tried to back away, to leave, but That Dude pulled her into a tight embrace and kissed her with the brutality of inexperience which Rose, in her naiveté, mistook for passion.

—⁓—

Pops pulled Rose by a chain around her ankle, into the kitchen and wound the other end around one of the legs of the old stove and locked her to it.

"I'm going to the police!"

Rose heard the sound of a motorcycle starting. Pops didn't notice.

"I don't see how. And even if you did, what would you tell them? That I locked you to the stove to keep you from going off with that thirty year-old dude? He's got nothing for you but welfare and suffering, Rose. Don't let a guy like that wreck your life."

Rose stopped fighting and deflated on the floor.

"And what do you have for me, Pops? Loneliness and heartbreak? Seems I can get that anywhere. There's loneliness and heartbreak on every corner. What if I want my loneliness and heartbreak with a man's arms around me, holding me tight and kissing me? I'm not sticking around here until it kills me like it did my mother."

"Not much you can do about it now, is there?"

Pops held up the keys to the lock and jiggled them at Rose before leaving her there in the dark.

Rose lifted the stove leg enough to slide out the chain and free herself.

Rose and I were the same age when we left Pops.

A year later, Rose was eight months pregnant and living in a small run-down apartment in Tulsa, Oklahoma. My father was packing his clothes in a saddlebag. He could hear the TV in the front room:

"Don't go liking Shane too much. He'll be moving on one day, Joey. You'll be upset if you get to liking him too much," Jean Arthur advised her son in an old western on TV.

My father put on his faded and worn black leather motorcycle jacket, picked up his saddlebag, and went into to the front room. Rose sat on the edge of the coffee table with her legs open enough to cool and dry her thighs in front of a fan. She took one look at my father with his packed saddlebag and said, "Good god, don't tell me Pops is going to be right."

Rose was a very alluring nineteen year-old, even looking like she swallowed a watermelon. My father had a tough time keeping his hands off of her.

"I never was much for stayin'," my father told Rose. "I told you from the start. You knew it all along what you were getting into."

"Baby, I meant it then and I mean it still, I love you exactly the way you are."

"I love you more than I ever loved any woman. I sure will miss you."

He stood her up and held her close so he could indulge in the smell of her skin and hair and memorize her face. She could not imagine life without him and began to weep. He cupped her face in his hands. Her running and smeared mascara became her tragedy mask. My father wiped his thumbs across her cheeks. He admired her gorgeous face one last time, kissed her on the forehead and left. Rose rushed to the door and watched that body she knew so well, as he walked to the chopper. She went in and shut the door where she could only hear him start the engine and drive away.

Rose hung in there with me for five years but grew increasingly restless. She obsessed over my father and an imagined life with us together as a family. Because of this, she never actually unpacked or settled into any of the places we lived in. She continued this way so long she developed strategies how to make it happen, how to bring us all together. She knew that the longer she sat around thinking about it, the less likely she was to find him. There were few people to track him. He moved too fast to be able to catch up with later. It was now or never.

5

At twenty-four, Rose set out in her cherry-red Volkswagen Beetle with me. It was a three-day ride to the pink stucco apartment building called The Arms where Pops lived next to a small aircraft junkyard. Before we left, Rose went for a manicure and pedicure with red polish to match the paint job on her car and shade of lipstick she always wore. She had put on her nicest, snug-fitting summer dress. I clutched my blankie for dear life. Under the smile she had going all day I felt increasing uneasiness.

Rose pulled up into the driveway of the Arms apartments and parked near the security entrance to the building. She turned to me and said, "You will never be alone, baby. Your grandmother watches over you. Your abuela, my mother, was named Concepción too. I named you after her. You are very lucky girl to have your abuela as your guardian angel. You will never feel alone or be afraid. She is always with you." Then she kissed the top of my head. "Want to come with me? I'm going over there to see if Pops is home."

I looked from her to the entrance and feared being that far from her at that moment so I scrambled out of the car when she came around and opened the door. I put my hand in hers and went with my blankie in the other hand. She pressed the intercom for his apartment.

"Who's there," was the gruff reply from the speaker.

"Pops, it's me, Rose."

There was a click and Rose knelt down to speak to me face to face.

"Pops is your abuelo, my father. He raised me himself."

I gripped her hand tighter and brought my blankie up to my face where I could hide in its scent. The door opened and out stepped Pops. He frowned at the sight of me. I moved in close and slightly behind Rose.

"Pops, this is your granddaughter."

"Where'd this event take place?"

"Tulsa. Listen, Pops, I have to make an emergency run to the corner market. Wait here with her for a sec and I'll be right back."

She put my hand in his and rushed over to the car. She pulled out a couple of trash bags of my clothes, toys, toddler supplies from out of the back seat and left them out on the lawn. Before she had finished, Blanche, Pops' neighbor, came out with a Polaroid camera on a strap around her neck. Blanche was in her early thirties then. She was an attractive woman and always on the lookout for a husband who could relieve some of the burdens of life as a single mother with seven year-old twins.

"Hello. Why, Mr. Burnes, who are these beautiful ladies?"

"Blanche, meet Rose, my daughter, and my granddaughter."

"You old devil," she said, with a wink and a teasing poke at his side. "I insist on a picture," she said, herding us together.

She took a Polaroid and kneeled down to show me the emerging image. I glanced at my mother.

"Go ahead, baby, it's an instant picture, see, it's magic."

Blanche let me keep the Polaroid. I am standing between my mother and Pops and holding their hands. Rose is smiling that convincing autopilot smile of hers that kept everyone happy. I'm looking up at her with a troubled expression. Pops looks into the lens, squinting in the direct sunlight, very gruff and generally masculine. Rose had slipped away while I watched the picture of us three emerge. She was in the car and started it up then leaned over to shout through the passenger window at Pops.

"I'll be right back."

I broke loose from Pops' grip and ran over to the car. Rose rolled up the window. I screamed indignantly and banged my fists on the glass. Rose leaned over to shout imploringly at Pops.

"Pops! Please."

Blanche came and took me by the wrist to the lawn and handed me over to Pops. Rose put the car in gear.

"Don't be longer than thirty minutes or I'm sending the dogs after you," Pops shouted at Rose.

This stiffened me with fear. I could not understand what dogs Pops might be referring to but it had an ominous tone to it. Rose leaned over to look me in the eyes.

"Remember, she is always with you, baby. I love you."

As Rose backed down the driveway, I screamed and broke out of Pops' grip to run after her. He snapped me back by grabbing my blanket and only then noticed the documents pinned to it. I let go and ran off. I watched as my mother turned a corner and disappeared from view then I broke down bawling out in the street.

Pops came and took me by the wrist and escorted me into his building, up an exterior staircase overlooking the open-air pool and into his apartment.

"You wait right over there on the sofa while I get your things," he told me, pointing.

I was torn between confusion and curiosity but sat down under the firmness of his command. He went right out and locked the door. I screamed and ran over to try and open the door but my hands were too small and slippery with tears and snot to get a grip on the knob. After giving up, I stood in the middle of the room with my blankie up at my face breathing it deeply.

Pops brought the bundles in and put them in a corner of the room then sat in a high wing backed chair near the front picture window. He pointed to the sofa and I obediently sat on it.

He put his feet up on an ottoman that had been elevated on stacked phone books to a comfortable height for him and studied me. I looked around to avoid that harsh stare. The ceiling was a drab and yellowed, previously white, stucco. The furniture was faded and worn. The single original lighting fixture was grimy and provided a dim yellow light.

"What does your momma call you? What's your name?"

"Concepción."

"Not anymore. See that picture on the wall over there by the dining table?"

I did not understand.

He went over and took a framed photograph off the wall and handed it to me. He sat back up on his throne and read through the papers that had been pinned to my blanket. I looked at the photograph in my lap. It was a picture of Concepción, sixteen years old, holding her mother's hand, Rosa Marie, who is very pregnant. Rosa Marie has her arm through her husband's, Señor Ramos. Armando, my great-uncle, stands stiffly at his father's other side with an expression of seriousness beyond his sixfteen years. Concepción's gaze was direct and compelling. Concepción smiled at me. It felt as though we had connected through time. Like she saw me.

"I'm going to call you Tulsa from now on because that is what your mother left to identify you."

"Concepción!" I corrected, folding my arms across my chest.

"From now on," Pops said, leaning toward me. "I will call you Tulsa Burnes. Be thankful you've got hands, feet, eyes and everything is working right. Be thankful you're with family. You get me, Tulsa?"

I dropped the photo and blankie and rushed to the door. I took hold with both free dry hands. It might have worked because I was getting a good grip but Pops stopped me by turning a bolt I could not reach.

"You sit back down," he commanded with an angry masculine authority unfamiliar to me.

"You will be well behaved until your momma comes back. I will not allow outbursts of any kind, you get me, Tulsa?"

I shook my head to be defiant.

"You will call me Pops, like your mother," he said impatiently. "And you will behave and live by my rules while you are here in my house."

Pops went into the kitchen. I noticed the dining room chair and climbed down off the couch to retrieve it so I could reach the lock. Pops heard the sound of the chair scraping on the linoleum floor as I dragged it across the dining room to the carpeted living room. I battled with him for the chair until he took it away and returned it to the table. I ran over to the sofa and sat down with my blankie up at my face and my thumb in my mouth.

"No thumb sucking. You better stay with me while I'm in the kitchen," he said, taking my hand and leading me in to where he made me sit on a stool. I watched him drop a tablespoon of finely chopped homemade chicken salad onto rye bread and press it down with a top slice. He handed it to me. I watched Pops cleaning up while I bit into it.

"No mas," I told him, handing it back. "Dónde está mamá?"

Pops took me through the living room into a bedroom. It was only large enough to accommodate a full sized bed, dresser, letter writing desk and a chair.

"This is where you will sleep while you are here. Now, in bed, pequeña, and I will tell you a story."

Pops put me in bed on top of the bedspread and covered me with the blanket I came with. He sat in a chair next to the bed and told me the old Yiddish folktale he would be telling me at bedtime for years after.

"Before the first child was conceived, it was determined that the infant in the mother's womb should lie like a closed book, its hands upon the temples, its arms upon the knees. The mouth is closed and the navel open. When the child is born, the mouth that was closed opens; the navel that was open closes.

Otherwise it would not survive even an hour. Just before birth a light is kindled upon the infant's head so bright it can see the world from one end to the other. Then another angel comes and teaches the infant the whole of knowledge and wisdom. That is the happiest day in the life of a human being.

But just before the infant leave's its mother's womb, another angel flicks its mouth on the center of the upper lip and causes to forget all it had learned. And that is why the upper lip is indented in the center. And that is also why people must find out again what they knew before birth and had been made to forget.

At birth, each infant promises, on oath, to do good and not evil; and is told that the soul is given them pure and it is their duty to keep it pure. If they fail to do so, they are warned that it will be taken from them. And that is how it has been since the first childbirth."

I woke up sometime later in Rose's arms. She was rocking me and gazing out the window, past brightly lit wrecked airplanes, toward something too distant to see. And she was quietly singing.

"You are my sunshine, my only sunshine," she sang in a hushed voice. "You make me happy when skies are grey. You'll never know dear how much I love you. Please don't take my sunshine away." I was snuggled in her arms, listening to her heart beat and drifting off. She sweetly sang, "The other night, dear, as I lay sleeping, I dreamt I held you in my arms. But when I woke dear, I was mistaken, so I hung down my head and I cried," and her voice cracked. My eyes shot open and I saw my mother weeping. She noticed me looking and sadly smiled at me. "My poor baby," she said to me and kissed my forehead. Then she rocked me again with my ear over her heart.

When I woke the following morning, I was alone in the bed. I panicked and climbed down off the bed and ran into the front room, frantically searching for her. I went into the kitchen where Pops was alone gathering bowls and two spoons for cold cereal. I ran into the empty bathroom.

I went into Pops' studio. Inside was a single futon, canvasses covered in chamois stacked against the walls,

studio light fixtures, an enormous easel, and paint supplies. I briefly forgot what I had been there to do and,
when it dawned on me, I ran into the living room and
burst into tears. Pops came over to me. He put his arm
around my shoulder and escorted me to the table where
he had set two bowls of cold cereal. He lifted me onto
a phone book he had put on one of the chairs for me.

"I'll make us some tea. You want tea?"

I didn't answer. Just sat there looking imploringly at
him and crying. He looked down and shook his head.
"What a damn shame," he said, shaking his head.

I wailed.

"Be a shame not to try this tea. Best you'll ever know."

The crying didn't stop but it did abate enough to sip
a cooled down version of sweetened chamomile tea.

6

One day, when I was eight, I entered the Arms Apartment's pool from the shallow end. I stopped a moment while I was still above water at the slope down into the deep end. The Arms pool was the first pool I had ever been in. Before there had only been full baths with clear water so I could submerge myself and look out. During many a bath I had wished to remain submerged and live in a muffled world of water where I could on occasion peer out at the strange dry world nearby.

Discovering the joys of the pool was a grand occasion for me. I told Pops all about it and I was so animated in the telling he became very attentive and interested in my descriptions of being submerged in water and the heady aroma of wet cement. But Pops wasn't with me when I went to the pool. I told him there was always an adult around but I made sure to go when everyone was at work or summer school or glued to their favorite soap operas so that no one was around.

On that day, when I stood on the tip of the slope down, I heard a crow caw and watched it fly overhead. I dropped under water and swam toward the deep end. At some point I looked up at a distorted female figure at the edge of the pool.

Next thing you know, I was alone in a walnut tree sitting next to an infant girl on one of the fat lower branches.

"Don't worry, it's going to be okay," the girl told me.

"Why, did something happen?"

"I've seen the whole of the world from one end to the other."

That's when I realized she didn't have dimple on her upper lip.

"Any advice? It's a big ocean and I'm only one girl in a little boat," I asked her.

"Yes my darling," the infant girl said. " Be always ready to say your goodbyes. As we leave we also meet and both are just as sweet."

For a moment I was in Rose's arms again. I even wondered if maybe I was dreaming, had been dreaming all along. I'm still eight but she was the same age and dressed exactly the same as that day she left me when I was five. She was singing to me. This time, instead of gazing out the window, weeping and never looking at me, she was looking into my eyes and smiling.

"You'll never know dear how much I love you," she sang, rocking me and stroking my hair.

It turned out to be Blanche's arms, next to the pool. I was soaking wet and she was holding a towel against my nose. It was full of blood. I must have passed out and she dove in to get me. She put my hand on the towel and said, "Don't let go." Then she picked me up and escorted me to her apartment.

There were others but I was barely aware of them, their voices sounded piped in. I tried to focus on Blanche's face. She kept eye contact with me as much as she could and smiled sweet Maraschino red and talked to me in a lovely almost lyrical voice about trying on French perfume and drinking chilled cherry Cool-Aid with a lemon slice on the edge of the glass and a thin clear straw. I nodded and nodded, smiling in gratitude.

She brought me into her bathroom and sat me at the edge of the bathtub. I watched her closely, that sweet face and lovely sincere smile. It warmed me up and made me ache for my mother. As Blanche tended to my dwindling bloody nose, I began to weep. Couldn't be helped. I had never been this close to mothering, or even this close to a woman since my mother left me.

"Oh my, what's going on here?" she asked and sat next to me.

I wiped the tears away roughly.

"You know what?"

I shook my head, dumbstruck by her cheer. It was like being smacked in the head by a blast of sunshine, which of course is what made it all the more tragic that she was condemned to raise her twin daughters, Denise and Debbie, who Pops nicknamed Double D. A shame because Double D successfully drained the bright light right out of her. You want to love someone but when the proposition includes witnessing that person's collusion in their own soul snatching you think twice. And though I didn't have as sophisticated an understanding at that age, I could see it.

That day she was inspired to ask Pops if I could stay for dinner so she could teach me how to make her special meatloaf. Of course he agreed. Whenever she made it she brought him a slice. He liked it so much he hardly noticed when Blanche told him I passed out in the pool. I watched all this through Blanche's front room window. Blanche turned around and looked at me with a perplexing amount of excitement. She came back in and led me to the old fashion vanity in her room and sat me on the stool in front of it.

"A lady always powders and perfumes," she explained while reaching for her fancy crystal perfume bottles with lovely tasseled diffusers. She sprayed and walked into the perfume mist. Then she sprayed in front of me and I leaned into the mist. It smelled like maternal comfort so deep and wide you never again see the cold light of day in the cruel world.

"Isn't it wonderful being a girl?"

I nodded. It was when I was with her.

She showed me how to make her meatloaf with such grace and cheer I could barely pay attention. When it was close to serving, Blanche had me wait at the dining table with Double D. They were sitting on one side and Blanche had set a place for me opposite and for herself at the head mostly so she could come and go serving and clearing. I sat down. Double D stared at me. They had this creepy way of staring at you while carrying on a conversation with each other.

"What were you doing exactly? Debbie asked me.

"She was trying to drown herself. She's having a nervous breakdown," Denise let her know.

"Are you crying?" Debbie asked me hopefully.

"You don't scare me," I told them both.

"Her mother just dumped her here like putting out the trash. Even had all her things in garbage bags," Denise told Debbie. "Guess her mother doesn't love her."

"Are you crying?" Debbie asks again, hopefully.

Blanche came to the table with a perfectly cooked meatloaf made in a Jell-O mold tin and decorated with catsup.

"How lovely, you are all getting acquainted. Here it is, my special meatloaf. The twins' favorite!"

Denise and Debbie rolled their eyes.

"When we were six," Debbie pointed out.

"Oh, I know you love it," Blanche responded, smiling at me. Undaunted. She winked at me.

"Bon appetit!" Blanche said, holding up her full fork and toasting with it.

Denise and Debbie looked at Blanche with naked disdain. Blanche made a clownish face to signal to me that she was amused.

"What is wrong with her?" Debbie asked Denise.

I caught the hurt pass almost imperceptibly over Blanche's face and then immediately she twisted her face into a clown mask. I couldn't bear it and walked out. I stormed to my room and threw myself on my bed. I refused to cry over them so I wiped the tears off my face.

Double D creeped me out but I didn't actually hate them until one night Pops finally invited Blanche over for dinner and Double D came with her. We had take-out Chinese food. After dinner I was instructed to play with Double D in my room while Pops showed his paintings to Blanche.

"He makes dirty pictures," Debbie told me.

"Doesn't he?" Denise demanded, stomping one foot emphatically.

"They are called nudes," I told them and sat down on the edge of the bed. Debbie picked up my Polaroid of Rose, Pops and me, looked at it and passed it to Denise.

"That's your mother?" Denise asked, looking at the picture then passing it back to Debbie.

"Not much of a mother. Where is she?" Debbie asked, tossing the picture on the bed.

"Are you crying?" Denise asked me hopefully, glancing at Debbie. They smiled.

"We're bored," Debbie said, heading for the door.

"Tell Blanche we'll be in our room," Denise commanded and followed her sister out.

The next day Pops and I were silently having our usual breakfast of cold cereal.

"Pops?"

"Yup."

"Why doesn't Blanche have a husband? She's so perfect."

"Nobody's perfect."

"Blanche is."

"Blanche is a good woman."

"Does that mean you'll marry her?" I had decided that once Blanche discovered what a loving daughter I was she would send Double D away.

"Blanche and I are good friends."

"You should marry her."

I had decided that I would make sure they got married.

"You should paint her picture, Pops. She's so beautiful."

And he did.

Blanche started coming over and staying late into the night while Double D remained in their room and I remained in mine. Blanche was transforming. Her stiff tight clothing loosened and her hair came down. She even smelled fresher, no more reeking perfume. Pops treated her differently than the other women who modeled for him. With the other women he was more formal and solicitous. With Blanche he seemed more himself, more the way he was around me. Except they laughed a lot together.

They became dear friends. I was convinced they would marry. Right after he finished her portrait, Pops spent a lot of time studying it. Then he put the last painting of Concepción next to the painting of Blanche and studied the two of them.

"This is why I paint, these two. At least I have something to show for all these years," he told me when I came in to give him his hot tea which I had been trained to prepare on schedule.

"Good ole Blanche. She's quite a lady." His words were like wedding bells.

I was excited over the wonderful life to come. I imagined us moving into a big house and Double D going to boarding school. I would remain in the local schools so that I could stay behind and provide indispensable help at home.

—⚏—

I was a loner at school but I had my skate buddy Geary to hang out with after school. He was older by three years but we got along and he didn't treat me like a girl, which I liked because it was altogether less condescending. Most adults underestimated how much I understood. Lack of experience is no hindrance to seeing through contrivances or phoniness or feigned superiority. In fact Geary and I often discussed this very topic.

"Adults suck," I said sitting next to Geary on a low wall.

"And they're dumb asses," he added.

We always met in the yard behind the abandoned "killing house," the neighborhood house where a tragic murder-suicide occurred.

The yard was overgrown, neglected and covered in blackened walnuts and since it was the house where a man murdered his family, nobody came around. All the windows were boarded up. Geary told me the family who once lived there was shot by the father who then shot himself. There are still blood stains in the floor.

We looked at the windows longing to go in and see the bloodstains while the goose bumps spread over our arms.

"How do you know?" I asked suspiciously.

"I saw it. When they first locked it up the windows weren't boarded so I looked in and saw all the blood stains."

"Why do you think he did it?"

"Because he hated his family."

Geary's aunt and uncle were raising him after his single mother died in an automobile accident. Geary's uncle owned a gun shop and was a big advocate. His aunt had a little sewing business out of the house. She always seemed harried and took outside smoke breaks every twenty minutes. Geary was left on his own most of the time. He made his own school lunches. He tried to help his aunt with her business but was only allowed to empty her trash and ashtrays or make her coffee.

When I got home it was long after dark. I walked into the apartment and faced Pops who was on his throne. He would have been painting but had been waiting for me.

"Thought I told you not to stay out with that punk after dark."

"You said 'late'," I corrected him on my way to my room. He followed me in.

"Do you mind?" I said indignantly.

"Listen here, kid, don't get an attitude with me. You won't ever go out with your skateboard again."

"What are you going to do, chain me to the stove?"

"No, I'll just destroy your board."

That scared me so I made sure to come home before dark for a while.

Then at dinner one night Pops was lecturing me about something I still can't remember.

"You get me, kid?" he asked as usual to make sure I was listening. I thought he was suggesting that I was too dimwitted to understand.

"You should know, Pops, you're as smart as you are tall and twice as world-wise," I quoted from something he had once said about somebody else.

"That's a lotta lip from a kid who can't even read a book."

"I can read."

"What is the last book you read?"

"Katie gets her first period. It came in that girls' first menstruation kit you gave me."

"Don't try to divert me with your shenanigans, kid. If you're going to be a smart-ass, better be smart."

He had thrown down the gauntlet. I was determined to read an adult book. The only hurdle was coming up with the money. It wasn't long before I went after the heirloom gold escudos. When I reached under his pillow for the coins, I felt cold metal and pulled out the Colt .45. It startled me and I fumbled and dropped it. I quickly grabbed a coin out of the bag and put the gun and coins back into hiding. I knew about the coins and heard stories about the pistol but I had never seen it. Pops had shown me the coins "in case anything happens to me, don't let anybody have these coins. They are yours on your eighteenth birthday."

Without a moment's hesitation I went straight away on my skateboard to the corner used bookstore.

It was the sort of bookstore that filled the walls from ceiling to floor with books stuffed into shelves and piles of books on the floor awaiting space on the shelves to open. I went in with my torn jeans, t-shirt, and disheveled hair. The cashier came around the counter to try and block me.

"Can I help you?"

I looked her up and down then went around her, giving her my back.

"No."

I went down the nearest aisle. I will show her I thought. I ran my finger across the spines of the books and stopped at a particularly thick one. I took it down and was immediately captivated by the picture on the cover of a ship in a stormy sea and the man trying to spear an enormous white whale. The man resembled Pops. I held on to the book and selected a narrow book from the opposite side of the aisle. It was a collection of 17th century English poetry. I cradled my first books lovingly in my arms up to the counter. The cashier glanced at them and examined me over her glasses.

"Well?" I asked

She checked for the prices. "Do you have money?" she asked me, crossing her arms.

I took out the gold coin and slapped it down on the counter and left without a bag or receipt.

I sat in the shade of a date palm on the corner by The Arms to look at the books. Though admittedly well-constructed older books have more heft to them than those first paperbacks I acquired that day, they never-the-less cast a spell over me. It was first and foremost the worlds inside and the degree of enchantment provided.

Then there was the tactile, sensory experience of touching a book, the smell of paper and ink, fresh and heavily laden with meaning. English poetry seemed "educated and well to do" as Pops would say. "English poetry," I said out loud. I found the title *Moby Dick* amusing. Then I opened the book of English poetry and there it was:

> *When the stars threw down their spears,*
> *And water'd heaven with their tears,*
> *Did he smile his work to see?*
> *Did he who made the lamb make thee?*

"When the stars threw down their spears and watered heaven with their tears," I said aloud, looking at the harpoon on the cover of *Moby Dick*. Not knowing the difference between a harpoon and a spear, I shivered from a sense of deeper meaning and eerie coincidence.

When Pops came home I was sitting at the table attempting to read *Moby Dick*. He came over and snatched the book out of my hands. He opened the cover and looked at the price.

"Where'd you get this?"

"Bought it."

"That so?" he said, putting it on the table. I picked it up and tried to look like I was searching for the last page I had been reading.

"You made me lose my page," I complained with some irritation.

"Where'd you get money like that?"

"I got it."

"How?"

"Borrowed it."

"Who from?"

"Myself."

Pops went straight to the coin bag.

"You said don't be a dumb ass!" I shouted down the hall after him.

He returned from the bedroom with the Colt .45 and sat at the table in his usual chair opposite me.

"Are you going to shoot me?" I asked, assuming a joke was forthcoming.

"I might at that," he said, checking the pistol probably to make sure it was not loaded but in my eyes he was checking to make sure it was loaded. Then he aimed it at me.

"You are going to read that book from front to back. Out loud."

"I will without the gun."

"You especially better with it," he said, cocking the pistol.

I opened to the first chapter and began reading.

"Call me Ishma–"

"Call me Ishmael," Pops corrected.

Reading *Moby Dick* was slow and painstaking at first. I could read at my grade level well enough but reading out loud at gunpoint was new to me. Pops constantly interrupted to correct me. In a few weeks I was reading more on my own mainly to keep his interruptions at a minimum. I figured out that more colorless speech put Pops to sleep after a while. I knew how long it took, what woke him up and for how long he would doze.

While he dozed it was easy to carefully go over and slip the pistol out from under his hand. I tried to open it the way Pops did to check for bullets, maybe take them, or something, but I did not know how. Pops stirred a little so I put it back under his hand and rushed back to my seat. I had the book open and was reading a passage.

"Back-up, I fell asleep," Pops said, raising his head, apparently unaware that the book was upside down. I feigned yawning and dropped the book on the floor. I picked it up and skipped ahead.

7

There was stillness to the white summer days when I was a kid. The air was still and fresh especially in the chaparral near where we lived. Higher in the canyons, the water ran past waterfalls and ended at the edge of our town, which spilled into a city of millions. Rigid streets led to the chaparral and the smooth meandering streets of the affluent wandered through it. The remaining yucca spotted the hills at development's edge where white blossoms leaned into the canyons to have a peek.

I stepped nimbly from rock to rock against the water's rush out down the canyon. When I was eight, the hike through the canyon was the thing to do. There were people there of all ages. I tried to go when there would be little to no one else around.

Deep in that canyon, high up into the mountain, there was a fresh pool five feet deep along a steep rock wall. Tucked here and there in that wall were tiny frogs that fit into the palm of your hand and were speckled slate and white like the stone they hid on. The pool was long enough to swim under water from one side to the other.

This was the place I went to after Pops had been keeping me reading *Moby Dick* at gunpoint for more days than I cared to count. I admittedly did develop a bit of a crush on the fictional tattooed and hairless savage, Queequeg, and that kept me reading to get to the parts about him. But I had to take a break so I went to the canyon to cool off. I was relieved to notice few others there.

There were the usual residents: beetles, dragonflies, an errant wasp, spiders, flies, and lizards. There was a coyote high up by the ridge scouting his next meal. It was all a lovely music to me. Just at the launch of a promising reverie, crows screamed in derision. It seemed like there were hundreds.

There might actually have been three. But one took a dive at me. I was certain they all had their attention on me. I shivered with a sudden chill running through the canyon. I stopped hiking and wondered if I should turn back. I couldn't think enough to figure it out or keep anything straight in my mind because of those infernal crows! I could have sworn they were cawing at me and dove at me whenever I started having a coherent thought. It pissed me off and I became more determined. So I continued and was able to put their screaming in the distance as I concentrated on hiking to the pool.

When I arrived at the pool, I was only then aware of the quiet. No crows. I looked around to make sure I was alone before taking off the shorts and t-shirt I had been wearing over my one-piece bathing suit. I put it all aside and walked into the water and dove under.

Only briefly while I was completely submerged was there any comfort. It lasted until I re-emerged and recalled I had to eventually go back where there was no comfort. I would have to return to where I felt uneasy and afraid of impermanence and not belonging. I came up near the rock wall and searched for a frog. It wasn't easy but when I found one, I studied it until it got nervous and dove into the water, away from me.

I was jealous of those frogs. Those little amphibians got to spend their lives right there in the grotto. I wanted a life in the grotto. I looked around at the eucalyptus trees, the poison oak along the sides of the canyon, yucca in bloom, protected by a moat of spears. I doubted I would ever feel at home anywhere else.

On my way out, as the canyon opened up, the sun was intense. I squinted and wondered if it had ever been that bright before. I saw crows flying high above as I made my way out of the canyon.

My eyes were slits against the harsh brightness. Everything seemed to crackle and pop. A lot of black ripe walnuts had fallen and carpeted the yard since I was last there in the back of 'the killing house." I heard the flapping of wings and watched the landing of crows high up in the walnut tree. I went across the yard to sit in the tree with them. The walnuts loudly crunched and cracked under my shoes.

"Matricide, killing your mother. Patricide, killing your father," I repeated from what Geary had told me once up there in the walnut tree after explaining what had happened at the killing house. I thought, killing your grandfather? "Pops-aside." I looked at the crows and imagined them cackling at the humor.

I ended up telling Geary everything that day, the coins, books, gun, and the Pops-aside joke, everything except the crows which he never noticed. He was very interested in the gun and coins, as a collector, he stressed.

"What kind of bullet does it take?" is what I wanted to know. Curiosity, I stressed.

"I would have to see it."

I took Geary into Pops' room the following day and pulled the Colt .45 out to show him. The coin bag fell off the futon onto the floor and I quickly put it back.

"Wow," Geary said, reaching for the pistol. "I can look it up if you want."

Geary checked to see if the pistol was loaded. It wasn't. I took it from him and put it back, hoping to leave the studio before Geary sees Pops' paintings. Just as Geary was about to lift a chamois on one, I stepped in front of him.

"I will show you my panties if you get me bullets for that gun."

"Show me now."

I slugged his arm.

Geary lifted a chamois and checked out the landscape underneath, one of the few from Pops' Paris days in a studio full of nudes.

The landscapes had something to do with his oeuvre as he explained it. I had no idea what that meant. I would roll my eyes and scoff at him every time he mentioned it. He would take me by the wrist to a closet and stand me there to watch him dramatically swing it open and pull out one of two traveling cases. He slid it over by me and slapped his palm over one of the many stickers that marked his exotic travels in the world.

"What sticker could be under here?" Pops asked me mockingly.

It was Paris, of course. He was there in the twenties. "Studying art," as he said.

This amounted to living in squalor in an attic, an ass kicking every night by the green faerie, Absinthe, and cursing life every morning. He was forced to paint out-door scenes for tourists, which meant fighting "those Parisian assholes" for a decent vantage point. He rotated his set-up at the city's popular spots, the tour Eiffel and Arc de Triomphe, all of the top selling spots that tourists buy from street vendors. He supplied them but it barely kept him fed and seldom did even that much. He was living a cliché that cut to his marrow more than squalor. In some mysterious manner, from a secret benefactor, Pops procured the funding to go back to the states and start again.

"Let me see," I said, playing along with his mockery of me. "It must be Paris, the worst experience of your life."

"Worst experience, most learning," he pointed out.

I figured that was only true for adults because they have such a difficult time seeing things as they are. With adults it's the past or even more grandiose, history, or the "if only" future, the one that you never accomplish because you never set out to do it. They "deal with" the present they do not live it.

Not kids. Kids live in the present where most things are new or at least not entirely familiar yet. I had no thought beyond making sure the gun was loaded for Pops' game. I was going to make my point at any cost. Pops would understand how dangerous this was.

"You have to wear a dress or no bullets," Geary said. "That's the deal. I'll be taking a big risk."

"Just get them," I said, holding my hand out to shake on it. "Pops says an agreement means nothing without a handshake."

Geary grinned and shook my hand. I slugged his shoulder.

"Owe!" he said, rubbing his shoulder.

"Perv."

I had kept the dress in my backpack all day at school and changed in the nearby gas station bathroom before meeting Geary. He was waiting for me by the walnut tree.

"Did you get them?" I demanded, cracking my way over.

He took one out of his pocket and held it up for me to see. I tried to take it but he kept it out of reach.

"What about our deal?" he asked, taunting me with the bullet.

"Okay, give me the bullets first," I told him, my hand out. He took the other one out of his pocket and dropped the two of them into my hand. He had cleared an area of walnuts so I spread my legs and held the bullet up to inspect in a ray of sun.

"Hurry up," I snapped.

Geary dropped down on his back and scooted under me to gaze up under my dress at my white cotton underwear.

I looked up at the metal casing of the bullet.

"When the stars threw down their spears," I quoted, "And water'd heaven with their tears, did he smile his work to see? Did he who made the lamb make thee?"

I heard Geary's zipper so I jumped aside and kicked him.

"Owe! That's not fair!"

"Fair enough you thieving pervert," I said on my way out of the yard.

That night Pops looked frantically for the Colt .45. When he came up to the table and saw me feigning to read *Moby Dick*, he knew something was up so he sat in his throne and waited. I stopped reading and put the pistol on the table. Then I put two bullets down next to it.

"What do you think you're doing?" he asked steadily.

"Better load it old man. You're a liar if you don't."

I picked up the pistol and loaded the bullets. Pops came over to stop me but I was able to load two of them in. In the scuffle the pistol went off, ripping through tendons and shattering bones in Pops' foot.

For a moment we both froze and stared at the red blossoming on his shoe. Pops gritted his teeth and sat down.

"Call an ambulance."

Pops made me stay with Blanche when they took him to the emergency room. Next day at school, government people interviewed me. They asked a lot of questions, especially about Pops' art. Had I ever been in the room with a naked woman? Has Pops ever exposed himself in front of me? Even after a shower? Stuff like that. They must have been satisfied with my answers. Pops always insisted on the utmost modesty, courtesy, and morality which I report as "Pops is a prude. Go figure." He is incapable of deceit or breach of trust in any way which usually comes out as "I feel guilty just thinking about lying around Pops." And the popular "I love Pops like a dad. He always has my back."

Again, from a mysterious source, Pops was provided a high priced attorney to insure custody of me until I turned eighteen. He even got his heirloom Colt .45 back.

For a week women from the building and the neighborhood brought their favorite dishes mostly as an excuse to meet Pops and see the paintings. I had to keep opening the door for them. On one particular day I remember, I breezed past Pops who held court on his throne to open the door for three of them.

"Look at you! So much more adult than they described on TV!" exclaimed the first one, handing me a Tupperware cake carrier as she went in to see Pops.

"Never blame yourself, honey," said the next on the heels of her chatty girlfriend who was already cooing and purring at Pops.

The third handed me a casserole dish. "Heat for ten minutes at three-fifty," she instructed, taking a last puff of a cigarette and handing it to me. I dropped the cigarette outside and crushed it under the toe of my shoe and shut the door with my elbow.

On another day, when I opened the door, fury blew a strange man in. He was a very big guy, over six feet and solid. He was wound up tight. He had the momentum of a man who had thought of nothing else for too long and stormed in ready to kill. As soon as this monstrous force saw Pops he stopped. He looked at me, confused.

"Burnes?" he asked Pops.

"Yes." Pops responded.

The guy was instantly deflated. He hung his head and walked back out. I shut the door and glared at Pops.

"Another husband?"

Pops shrugged and wrote in chalk on a little chalkboard: "I ask if their husbands or boyfriends mind the modeling first but the ladies always lie."

And then little chalkboards went up all over the apartment. He never addressed me directly or told me the bed time story, or provided any guidance. Never a word after I shot him.

I was Pops' nursemaid for months while he recuperated. He kept his foot propped up and prominently on display. I did everything. Blanche took me to the store and helped me buy the groceries. She taught me simple meals. I thought Pops would eventually speak to me when his foot was better and he was no longer in pain. He started writing me notes and had me buy stacks of chalkboards for essential little communiqués like, "Bring me my tea."

I asked Blanche to talk to him but she didn't want to tell Pops how to raise me any more than she wanted Pops to tell her how to raise Double D.

Blanche lost her luster.

In the years of Pops silence and Blanche's demoted status everything lost its luster.

Geary got out of the youth detention facility the year I turned fourteen. He was seventeen. Hair grew on his face and all his friends were older. I was still skating and Geary drove a truck. His uncle gave him a truck in an attempt to appease Geary's aunt. She had been embarrassed by the negative attention Geary's uncle was receiving for his parenting especially the part where he made Geary work in the gun shop too young against labor laws. The deal was Geary had to go to school or get a job. I would see him drive by while I skated to and from The Arms. We did not acknowledge one another at first. Then we ran into each other at the local mini-mart.

"Hey, Tulsa."

"Hey Geary. Are you mad?" I asked him.

"Not anymore."

"They already had it figured out. Everybody knew we hung out and your uncle has a gun shop."

"I know."

"I'm sorry you had to go in there."

We sat in his truck for a while sipping super-sized sodas and sharing nachos.

"What was it like in there?"

"There were kids in for murder."

Geary even smelled different. I looked at the hair on his chin and blushed. Geary had a good look at me, too. I was wearing a bra by then and I had grown taller.

"You been kissed yet?" he asked me, checking out my developing chest.

"No."

"You have to kiss me to get out of this truck."

I tried to open the door but Geary stopped me. He was much bigger and had been working out.

"Just one kiss."

"Let me go."

"Not until you kiss me."

I kissed his cheek and tried to open the door again. He stopped me and pinned me against the seat.

"Open your mouth like this," he told me and demonstrated by parting his lips a little.

I was frankly curious about kissing and thought it couldn't hurt even though Geary would not normally be my first choice for first kiss. This was more like research, I told myself, and parted my lips.

"Stay like that," he said then pressed his lips against mine. When he stuck his tongue in my mouth and moved it around I squirmed away. He laughed and reached across me to open my door.

"Next time you're gonna kiss back."

"No I'm not," I shouted after I had gotten out and slammed the door. Geary burned rubber taking off, covering me in a noxious cloud.

"Dick-head!" I shouted after him.

I heard later from kids around the neighborhood that Geary became a speed addict. Eventually you could tell just by the sores on his face and his rotting teeth.

—⚬⚬⚬—

I read a lot since the shooting accident. I was too uncertain about making friends with other kids after Double

D and Geary so I was alone all the time and constantly in the library. I read fiction voraciously to momentarily liberate me from a grim home life.

It wasn't enough, though. I was going to have to go. And traitor Blanche was going to help me. She had always been concerned about Pops nude painting of her somehow being seen by anyone. She wanted him to keep it safely in his room and covered. One day, when Pops was at work and Double D were at horseback riding class, I took the painting over to her apartment and knocked on the door. Blanche opened it and smiled, delighted to see me.

"Why, Tulsa, what a lovely surprise. What brings you to my door?"

"We have to talk."

We went inside and sat down.

"What do you have there?" she asked pleasantly.

I removed the chamois and revealed the painting.

"What are you doing with that?" she asked, sitting forward.

"I'm going to show it to the neighbors unless you give me a thousand dollars."

"A thousand dollars? For what?"

"That's not important. Just decide if you want everybody to see this or not."

Blanche shook her head. "Tulsa, if you are in some kind of trouble, let's figure a way out together. You don't have to blackmail me to be your friend."

"You're not my friend. You let Pops ignore me for years. Call it abandon tax."

Blanche put her hand over her cheek. "Has it been that long?"

"What's it going to be, Blanche?"

"Tulsa, I'm sorry, but I don't care anymore whether that painting is seen and I don't have that kind of money. I'm paying for the girl's education. I don't even have enough for groceries sometimes."

I wept furious tears. How come the despicable Double D get to have a self-sacrificing mother when they treat her like dirt? I hated them. I hated Pops. He might as well have let me out by the side of the highway. I went home and shredded the painting then left it on Blanche's doorstep. Later, while I was reading in my room, there was a knock at my door. Blanche came in. I could see Pops behind her, peering in to have a look at me. Blanche sat on the edge of the bed.

"What did Pops say about your picture?" I asked bitterly without looking up from my book.

"He doesn't know yet."

I looked up.

"He told me once that that painting was one of the most important to him. I didn't have the heart to tell him."

"Speaking was important to me."

"I have been very caught up in work and taking care of the girls. I just lost track of what was going on outside my own home, I guess. I realize now I could have said something back then, or kept at him, maybe. I'm sorry, Tulsa... Friends?"

That hurt me more. She was wrapped up in her own life, huh? What kind of a friend is that?

"Will you give me the money, then?"

"Tulsa, I honestly don't have it."

—◦◦◦—

I had started reading in a local coffee house just to have a place to go aside from the apartment and library. I practiced the Rose act. I smiled a lot and was generally friendly with anyone no matter what I really thought of them. It was a winning manner. I quickly made a lot of friends. The baristas and regulars at the cafe befriended me and I was soon a part of the little community there. I was eventually hired and trained as a barista.

I began watching the community bulletin board for roommate wanted notices. Then, not long after my seventeenth birthday, I saw a notice for a room in a three-bedroom apartment to share with four other people. I met them and they liked me. They said I could move in anytime. All I needed was a cash deposit. I had been saving money so I went straight home to pack up one of Pops' traveling cases with a few things.

Pops caught sight of me packing on his way past my room. I stopped and looked at him. He stood where he was and pushed the door open a bit more to a good look at what I was doing. He looked me in the eye then went into his own room. When he went out for the mail, I took the old monadero full of gold out from under the pillow. I put it on top of the clothes I had packed along with the Polaroid and the picture of Concepción. Then I left without saying goodbye.

8

I thought about Pops now and then. I'd look at a sticker on the old traveling case of Veracruz or Cuba and envy the freedom and possibilities he had early in life. Nothing about the world was the same, not for men or for women. It wasn't as safe. But neither was staying in one place for very long and collecting scars from the emotional damage.

I was always the tourist, the traveler. I was clueless how to interact with anyone personally or intimately, so I stayed away from intimacy with guys. And I waded through the shallow end of friendly with women. I never acquired more than what I left Pops' carrying and never returned to most places. There were no deep and lasting friendships. No tears. I was lovely to everyone but, just like the yucca tree, I had a moat of spears to keep them from my more beautiful and delicate parts.

After a couple of years it was routine, almost a habit, to float around like that. But it promised nothing. Desire creeps in and next thing you know you are imagining that you can have a home and family like everyone else. It was at this point of dissatisfaction with my lot that I arrived at the cottage at the age of twenty-five.

Linda had been living there. I didn't even know Lance yet. Linda was ten years older and had an edge to her but a lovely and charming manner. I met Linda at Beef Corral where we worked. When I started, she had already been there for years. I admired her familiar way with the place, with everyone who was there. I also liked that she was a rescuer.

One day, after I had been employed there for a week and been eyed by everyone, Hector, the manager, waved me over.

"Tulsa, you like meat?" he looked me squarely in the eye as if he had just asked if I liked ice-cream.

"Do I like meat?" I glanced around wondering if anyone else was in on this or could give me a clue.

Linda, distracted from her lunch, poked her head up over a booth.

Hector smiled and waved Linda away. "I'm not asking you, Linda, I already know you don't."

Linda shook her head like she was accustomed to Hector's double entendres.

Hector, in a grand gesture, pulled out a stainless steel drawer that was big enough to fit a human corpse. He indicated he wanted me to come closer and have a look. It was full of stacks of plump steaks—the remains of a slaughtered cow.

Linda was all of a sudden by my side, taking my arm. "That's a lot to live up to, Hector, careful you're not giving women too high an expectation of yourself," Linda said, leaning into me as though we were sisters sharing a joke. I liked that Linda acted like we were a team.

"Here," she said, sitting me down at the booth and grabbing a bowl and spoon for me. "Have some granola."

"Thanks. Are you a vegetarian?"

"Thirteen years. You?"

"Uh, thirteen minutes."

She chuckled. When she asked me about myself she seemed truly interested.

"I live in a downtown building that's about to be torn down in favor of condos and I've been out of work too long to save enough money to move."

It was mostly true. I was being evicted from a loft paid for by two people I hardly saw and didn't know very well. I had no one and no place to go. I had spent the last five years moving from place to place. It had been easy meeting people and finding places to stay for a little while but I never kept in touch and this time it was down to the wire.

"You're coming home with me," she declared, reaching over and taking my hand. Milk and granola spilled out of my spoon onto the table. "We can pick up your things later. You have a lot?"

"No, um, I don't, but are you saying I can move into your place?"

Linda grinned and nodded.

Wow, I thought. She's almost too-good-to-be-true kind and friendly. Must mean trouble.

Linda pulled her small flatbed truck up in front of the nondescript former sweat factory I had been staying in on the edge of downtown. I was waiting out front and tossed Pops' stickered-up travel case onto the flatbed.

"You weren't kidding," Linda said, swinging into the crowded downtown traffic. "My shoes take up twice that room," she boasted, smiling.

I watched through the back window as the building I had lived in receded behind us.

"What size do you wear?"

I looked down at my Doc Martens. No way was I going to collect purses and shoes, I told myself. Not ever.

"Eight, I guess. I don't make a habit of buying shoes."

"Time you did. At least a few."

"I like to keep my stuff at two check-in and two carry-on."

"Life isn't a frequent flyer program, Tulsa. It's okay to have a life, you know."

"I do, life light. L-i-t-e."

When we arrived at the cottage, she presented an old army cot to me. She had been using it in the little front room for seating. There was a narrow futon on it. It was sturdy and wide enough to make a bed for me.

"It's what I've got. You're welcome to pick-up something else."

I put my case and clothes down on the floor next to the cot and sat on the edge, which didn't give. "This is great," I said with contrived zeal.

"I'll make room on my clothes rack." She went to the room in back and waved me over. The narrow room was lined with shoe racks filled with various styles. A couple clothing racks held what looked like a summer wardrobe. She had made the room her walk in closet. She shoved aside some clothes and cleared half of one of the racks for me.

"Do you think it'll be enough? I can make more room if you need it. Just let me know, okay? It's no problem, so don't be afraid to ask. You can wear anything of mine you want. Don't even have to ask."

I felt Linda's life opening up to swallow me and choke.

She got a thrill out of having an audience for her elaborate dress up sessions. I hung out in her bedroom the two or three hours while she got ready to go out. I watched as she powdered her skin from neck to toe and tried on a series of outfits.

She'd ask my opinion rhetorically like, "Too loose?" "Not flattering enough?" and "Too hoochie momma?"

I just repeated, "too loose," too whatever. She would pull clothes down off the rack she had in her room and try them on in front of the mirror, wait for her echo, then toss them on the bed. I made myself useful by picking them up and returning them to the rack.

"Why don't you come with me?" she asked the first two nights. "You can meet Vinnie. We'll be backstage."

"Next time," I kept telling her. But then, one night, she insisted on dressing me up and putting makeup on me. I thought maybe she just wanted to parade me in front of people as her creation. I could play that.

We began to go together every time her rock idol boyfriend Vinnie played guitar in garishly lit, small and crowded clubs over ripe with the stink of beer and sweat. She took me to raves and gave me psychotropics and told me, "Life is not a trick played on you. It isn't something that happens outside of you that you are a victim or witness of. It is a force in you."

I wondered if maybe she was just spiritual enough to be for real.

Everything was going smoothly. It was a good set-up until Vinnie started coming around the cottage more and staying with her behind the closed door of her bedroom.

No more late night hot cocoa and catty giggling. No more dressing up together in her room.

That first night he stayed over, I was lying stiffly on my army cot reading, trying to focus despite the laughing and moaning a few feet away on the other side of that door. I couldn't focus on the book I was reading so I stared at the ceiling. There it is, I thought, the ceiling. This ceiling is the ceiling in my bedroom when I was a kid. This ceiling is all there is in the world. I will be lying alone staring at a series of ceilings for the rest of my days while others interact and know each other in ways that will always elude me. Linda giggled. I closed my eyes, hoping sleep would miraculously pluck me out and take me away.

There was a knock at the front door. More of a rap, actually.

I tensed with the anticipation of Linda coming out of her room to open the door. The stereo went on in Linda's bedroom and a track from Vinnie's album began a torturous muffled thumping against the wall.

I went over to the window to peek out and saw him, saw Lance for the first time. Lance looked to be around my age, tall and lanky with light brown eyes and scraggly hair. He looked toward me with that friendly smile of his and I didn't hesitate to open the door. When he saw me he reacted the way people usually do and stared but he quickly composed himself.

Pops had warned me about it. "Beauty blinds men, Tulsa, they won't be able to truly see you but they will always want their hands on you."

And kids will tease you into a neurotic, he should have added. I might have seen it coming. I was teased for being so white. I was called "wonder bread." Milk was poured over my head. I was called "bug eyes" and often had my long braid yanked by boys. While suffering the constant torment of the kids around me, I had nervously plucked out all of my eyelashes and they have never grown back.

"Hi," Lance said, noticing the book in my hand. "Is Linda here?"

"She's kinda busy."

"We haven't met," he said with that smile of his.

"I'm the new lodger," I said in an almost self-mocking tone.

He put out his hand to shake. "Nice to meet you, lodger, I'm Lance," he took my hand and kissed the back of it. Oh brother, I thought. But he had a way of smiling that let you know he was amusing himself. Well, okay, I thought, he might be all right.

I opened the door wider. "Would you like to come in?"

"Thank you, what should I call you, Lodger?"

"Tulsa."

He walked in and waited to sit down.

"Why not Carolina or Reno?"

I gestured for him to sit in the overstuffed chair. He sat down and put his pack on the floor.

"Tulsa works best if you want me to answer."

"Okay, Tulsa."

He loved reading Henry Miller and went through a Beat phase. He claimed to have read *Ulysses* and *Gravity's Rainbow* all the way through. He wanted to talk about Aldous Huxley and George Orwell.

"*Brave New World* is more prophetic than *1984*," he explained, "Because Aldous Huxley had expanded his mind on hallucinogenics and could see society hurtling toward mind-numbing non-stop entertainment."

"Entertainment alone only anesthetizes minds. You have to add a propaganda strategy to maneuver the crowds where you want them. Orwell was just as prophetic as Huxley," I added.

He looked around the room. "Where is your television?"

"Ha, really," I said.

Linda must have heard us because she poked her head out of her room. "Lance. I didn't know you were here. What's going on?" she asked him.

"Hey, Linda," he said, "I told Tulsa not to bother you but invited myself in for a minute."

"Fine," she said, returning to her room and essentially shutting the door in our faces. I looked at Lance. He shrugged.

"Tea?" I asked Lance on my way to the kitchen.

"Okay," he said. We heard Vinnie laughing.

"I take it she's not alone," he said, smiling.

"Do you know her boyfriend?" I wondered how much to say on the subject.

"I met him."

"Linda is losing her head over him," I said shaking my head and leaning back against the refrigerator to wait for the kettle to boil. Lance was amused.

"What?" I asked, embarrassed and not knowing why.

"What's wrong with Linda losing her head over somebody?"

"It's not that, I wish he would keep to the basics with me like 'hi' and 'bye'. It's making her crazy."

"What about music?" Lance asked me.

"I don't have any of that right now."

"What do you do?"

"Read, mostly."

Lance and I whispered together into morning talking mostly about the books we loved. My eyelids became heavy after midnight but I wanted to sit there near him, whispering and stifled laughter forever. I learned that Lance had rock climbed in the Himalayas, parachuted over the Mojave, and had worked in an Alaskan fishery. When it became obvious to Lance how sleepy I was he slowly packed up. It took an hour before he got to the door.

"Tulsa," he said as if trying out the sound of it. "I never asked you how you got that name."

"My grandfather."

"Are you from Tulsa?"

"I was born there."

"Well, I'm glad you're here now."

"Thanks, Lance."

9

I wasn't a virgin when I met Lance but nearly so. My few sexual encounters were collisions with strangers best forgotten. Lance was the first person I felt at ease with and we quickly became friends. That night, when our hands accidentally touched while I handed him tea, I felt a jolt of desire for him. Something I had never felt before.

I wasn't quite sure what was happening to me but I had the impression he was experiencing something too because he looked me in the eyes whenever it happened. My arms ached when Lance left as if it would be a terrible tragedy never to hold him. I almost hoped I would not see him again because it frightened me. I couldn't help thinking about him and listening for his rap at the door.

—ᴍ—

I didn't notice it at first but Linda's personality was changing. She didn't like Vinnie talking to me or spending any time near me. But she continued to stock his favorite beer in the refrigerator and let him come out to retrieve it himself. He had to pass me coming out and going in. I made sure to have books at hand so that even if I'm not reading I can still pretend.

After a few weeks of Linda growing increasingly surly, not inviting me to go out on the weekend, ignoring me at work by pretending she was engrossed in someone or something else, I realized my charm was not going to retrieve her from the distance she had already traversed. I could only watch her go and wonder where I would be living next.

If that weren't bad enough, one night Vinnie came out of Linda's room in nothing but his boxers. I had been falling asleep while reading. When he opened Linda's door, it startled me awake. I caught the book from falling and saw his back after he had passed me. I looked over at Linda's open door. I was stricken with discomfort at the sense of Linda's unseen presence in her bedroom, listening for Vinnie's return. I turned to the wall with the book in front of my face. Vinnie plucked a beer out of the fridge and sat down in the stuffed chair next to the cot. A terrible dread landed in my chest.

"Any good?" he asked, popping open the beer and taking a drink.

"Mmhmm," I said, not moving and wondering what book I was holding up at my face.

"I like that about you, Tulsa. You're always reading."

He can't really be telling me what he likes about me.

"It's my favorite affectation," I told him, sitting up because I was not about to hang out lying down.

"No, come on, you're no fake."

"Guess I've perfected it, then."

"Vinnie?" Linda said in a sweet voice.

And back he went into her room behind the closed door. I let out a long sigh and wondered how long I had been holding my breath.

Then one night, while Linda was out adoring Vinnie in his band at a show, Lance finally returned.

I leapt up and opened the door for him. He was carrying a portable player and his filled backpack and smiling broadly.

"Music," he said, lugging it in.

He set the player up near the cot and pulled a stack of CD's out of his pack. He played French hip-hop jazz.

"You know I don't understand French, right?"

"Don't worry, I'm enjoying it enough for both of us."

"Are you French? Where were you born?"

"Technically I am a citizen here but my family is from France, yes. How about you?"

"Mexican and extraterrestrial. Tea?" I asked him on the way to the kitchen.

"Okay, yeah, now I see it in the bone structure," he said, following me in. "How's everything on the Linda front?"

"Same. How is everything with you? Don't you live in your own place?"

"Well, yeah, but I don't know how much longer."

"Thanks for the tunes."

"I had to bring it. Wouldn't come otherwise."

"Oh, thanks."

"I'm used to being in a house filled with people."

"You have brothers and sisters?"

"I'm an only child."

"Okay."

"There were always people who worked in the house. How about you? Brothers or sisters?"

"None that I know of."

Having an actual friend for the first time inspired more enthusiasm in me about my life, which wasn't otherwise improving. At least I had a confidant in Lance. I kept him abreast about the Linda drama and how my days left in the cottage were diminishing. I was secretly hoping he'd invite me to his house. She didn't like that I was taking her buddy Lance from her. She began ignoring me, not easy considering we worked and lived together.

Linda would silently come out of her room to zap a dinner in the microwave or snatch flatware for take-out food then ignore me on her way back behind that closed door. Since I lived in the front room she had to maintain that river of silence coming and going. It was not having the effect on me that I think she had hoped.

I'm guessing my utter lack of concern bothered her the most because she started slamming cabinet doors, the bathroom door, her door, the front door. She had it in for the doors. The less I was affected the more she slammed doors. She became so frustrated she started carrying on angry conversations with herself in her room. Pops had stopped speaking to me to make a point. He was silent for years because he was astoundingly stubborn. Linda's motive was unfamiliar and eventually unsettling. I had no idea what to expect so I finally did feel edgy when she was around.

She made sure the manager at Beef Corral scheduled us for different shifts. He thought it was funny because she used to make sure he scheduled us together. She turned the other waitresses against me by telling them that after she took me in when I had no place to go I was flirting with her boyfriend and stealing her friends. She was obviously hoping to force me out of her life. I would gladly oblige but I didn't have any money. I couldn't save money because I wasn't making enough and didn't own a car. I dreaded looking for another job on the bus.

I was beginning to feel uncomfortable with how poorly everything turned out with Linda. Thanks to her I got that job. When I had first walked into Beef Corral I had been looking for work and making the rounds for weeks. When Linda walked up to me in the uniform of skimpy white pleather skirt and calf-high white cowboy boots, both with fringes, I giggled. She looked down at her clothes and giggled with me. I asked for an application and she was only too happy to give it to me. She told me to put her down as a reference and went over my application so she could appear to know me. She wanted at least one other waitress in there who had a sense of humor.

Working there now was distressing. A feeling of lost equilibrium tormented me. I started dropping things and bumping into furniture and customers. I entertained the idea of apologizing, begging her forgiveness, shaving my head to repel Vinnie. Tell her anything to restore balance and peace, I told myself. I decided when I next see her I would supplicate at her feet. I had never done it but I had never lived under an overpass either. However hard it might be it could not be as hard as a concrete bed.

A great sense of relief left me feeling more uplifted. I was certain everything would turn out as I imagined. I was completely off my guard when Hector asked to see me in his office after I closed everything and clocked out.

Hector was about thirty and maybe five-foot six. I didn't think of him as good-looking with his paunch and mustache but a few of the girls were very flirty with him, which never ceased to baffle me.

The shelves and floor in his office were crowded with supplies for the restaurant and the desk was a mess of papers. There was a framed picture on it of a woman posing with a boy and girl, both toddlers. He asked me to sit down and I took note that he looked to see if anyone was around before shutting the door. He had a rule we all learned on our first day that no one was to enter his office when the door was closed before knocking and being granted permission. Hector came over and sat on the edge of the desk.

"What's up, Hector?"

"That's what I wanted to ask you, Tulsa."

"What do you mean?"

"Tulsa, you've been a good waitress and I don't have any complaints but I can't have you girls fighting or letting your personal life interfere with the work."

"How is it interfering?"

"What happened with you and Linda?"

"What did she tell you?"

"Why don't you tell me?"

"Nothing that will interfere with my work, I promise you that, Hector."

"You're a nice girl, I like you. But this business between you and Linda has to end. I don't want to, believe me, but I will have to let one of you go and it'll have to be you."

"Hector, I don't make enough to save. I could get a second job but it will take time."

"Perhaps I can help you there. A few of the girls make extra money after hours. You could make up to a hundred a week if you wanted to. How's that sound?"

"Really?"

He nodded and smiled. I was excited. I could save enough to move in three months. "What's the job?"

"You can't tell anyone, it would be between us."

"What is it?"

"Between us?"

"Okay."

"Well, for example, one girl helps me keep my stress down. It only takes maybe fifteen minutes. If you did that four times a week I'd pay you a hundred dollars."

I felt ill.

"You're a beautiful girl. That's in your favor." He began to bulge under his pants and adjusted himself. I stood up.

"We're only talking about a little hand job here and there."

I looked at his family photograph and had to keep myself from breaking it over his head.

"Wow, Hector, I appreciate you trying to help me. Mind if I sleep on it?"

He looked a little flustered. Maybe he thought he was going to get a hand job there and then.

"Let me know tomorrow," he said, opening the door. I left without looking at him.

10

T he world was looking ugly to me then. Life was grim and yielded only torturously brief moments of happiness. It was clearly time to be submerged. It had been too long. The bathtub in the cottage was three-quarter the size of a real bathtub. I tried filling it and dunking my head but that was clearly inferior and speaks volumes how desperate I was. It had not necessarily been the water that comforted me so much as being sub-merged released me. When I was at the height of my need to submerge there was that familiar rap at the door.

Lance came bounding in full of vitality and next thing you know we were on our way to a rave at a ware-house by the beach. We drove through all the sparkling towers of commerce and industry downtown.

Lance faced fiercely foreword, heavily concentrated on the traffic. He grew more unfamiliar as the ride went on by the length of his lack of attention to me. That was when I first became aware that when he wasn't paying attention to me it felt like a deficit, like something which took up a lot of room had suddenly vacated.

As you approach the coastline there is a definite change in the air. You would know blindfolded when you were near the ocean once you're familiar. I rolled down my window to smell the air.

You could not tell from outside the upscale business building that the inside walls are painted black and people gathered with florescent paint to play with and plenty of live music to move their bodies to. The crowd flowed in the space phenomenally well considering how packed it was. And it literally sucked me inside. I gave myself to it and let the crowd pull me into the main room. I felt their hands, arms, chests, and sides all over my body and my head tingled from it. I felt the rhythm of the music under my feet before I heard it. The further into the building I went the more intoxicated I was by it all. Then I looked up.

Heads above the crowd was this towering creature. I say creature for the sexually ambiguous tall thin frame revealed no clues. The face was long and jaw strong, almost masculine. I admired the shredded, discolored and faded corset hugging that frame. I think maybe female. Her platinum dreadlocks animated like wild albino serpents. She went with her entourage around her to the stage. They all proceeded to pick up an instrument and when her lamenting into the microphone began, they accompanied her with sweet, painful music.

I was pulled into the tightly packed vortex of dancers. And there I remained, dancing. I lost track of time, location and concern for any of it. I was separated from the outside world. It couldn't penetrate. It would not reach me here. Of course I had no idea where Lance was but it occurred to me only briefly once during the night. When the place was mostly cleared out of people at three in the morning, I finally ran into Lance. Turns out he knew the singer. Her name was Daria. She had invited him. All this I learned during the chatty drive back home. Never once did he ask me how my night went, what I had seen or experienced. It prickled at the back of my mind.

Lance dropped me off.

Linda wasn't there so I was thankfully alone in the cottage. I took the opportunity to drink a cup of tea comfortably in the chair. While I sat there sipping tea, I pictured that towering frame moving through the crowd. Her bravura reminded me of Pops. I recognized that instinctively fine sense of theater. People like that have a talent for lifting you out of the mundane world and permitting you a bit of their enchantment. I wished I could enchant people that way. I think I've only perfected an ability to captivate attention. But to truly enchant, now that was magic.

I tried to think of what I had an instinctively fine sense of. I had a sense of retributive fervor. I imagined two big guys beating the crap out of Hector. I visualized them holding Hector down so I could have a go at him myself. I wanted to report him but I couldn't lose my job. I figured there was only one thing I could do.

The following night I called in sick and dipped into my rent money to hire a taxi and wait in it for Hector to leave work. I followed him to his middle-class home. He had to move a tricycle out of the driveway before entering the garage. I imagined his son running out of the house, excited to see him, a boy who was likely to have the same disdain for women in his life. I wrote down Hector's address then had the driver take me home.

When I came in, I heard that god-awful music thumping against the wall in Linda's room and a familiar heaviness descended on me. For hours I lay on the cot with my arm hanging over the edge holding the paper I had written Hector's address on, staring at the ceiling.

Then there was that telling rap at the front door. I hid the paper under the cushion of the chair before opening the door for Lance. I shuffled back in.

"What happened?" Lance asked.

"Tea?" I asked on my way to put the kettle on.

He came and leaned in the doorway.

"What happened? Linda?"

"I'm just tired from work."

"I can come back some other time,"

"It's okay. Have tea before you go."

"No rest for the wicked, huh?"

"No rest for the weary."

The next night I went to work smiling at Hector as if he were in for a treat. He seemed pleased. After closing the restaurant, I asked him if I could see him in his office and we went in. Hector closed and locked the door behind us then sat on the edge of his desk, grinning. I smiled back.

"Hector, I came up with an arrangement suitable for us both."

"Good," he said, beginning to unzip his pants.

"Hold on, tiger. Let's go over things and shake on it."

"Whatever you say," he said, rubbing himself.

His face was puffy, red, and slick with sweat. A picture of the scrunched faces he made when he was having an orgasm kept flashing through my mind and I strained to keep from laughing.

"It's simple," I told him "You give me the equivalent of my weekly pay and I will stay home and not go to five-five-six-one-zero Alta Vista Drive to tell your poor wife what you have been doing here."

Hector almost lost his balance jumping up and zipping his pants. He grabbed my shoulders and shoved his red face so close to mine I could smell onion on his breath.

"You can't prove anything. Out, puta!"

And he shoved me through the door.

"I'll let you sleep on it, Hector," I yelled back to him.

When I arrived home, Linda and Vinnie were loading her things onto her truck. I stood outside watching for a moment. Vinnie glanced at me. Linda came out with a crate of dishes.

"Linda, what's going on?"

"Isn't it obvious?"

"You're just going to leave me here with an empty place and all the rent?"

"Isn't it time you got your own things?" she said then loaded the crate and ignored me as she passed to go inside the cottage. Vinnie passed and avoided looking at me. I followed them in and almost lost my footing when I saw how bare the place was. The cot, chair, and my case, were all still there but little else. There were a few dirty dishes in the sink and the trash was full. Vinnie cornered Linda in the other room. They whispered and then started arguing.

"I'm not giving her my money," Linda said raising her voice. Vinnie tried to shush her and whispered something else. She stormed out with another box and Vinnie came over and slipped a roll of cash in my hand. He put his finger over his lips before walking out. I counted sixty bucks.

"Is it too late to say I'm sorry?" I shouted after them. "And ask to borrow your half of the rent?"

They ignored me. That was it. I was in a deep fix. I called Lance.

"Lance," was how he answered the phone. "Lance," he repeated.

"What's the worst thing that could happen to me right now aside from being physically harmed? Can you guess?"

"Tulsa?"

"Linda's clearing out."

"I'll be right over."

Lance showed up at the end of Linda's cottage-haul-away. I was standing in the doorway, watching Linda and Vinnie finish up.

"Hey, Linda, Vinnie," Lance said, sizing up the situation.

"Lance," Linda and Vinnie said simultaneously.

"Shacking up?" Lance said, smiling, trying to introduce some levity.

"Changing the scenery," Linda told him with a glance in my direction.

"How are you doing, Tulsa?" Lance asked.

"I've been better, thanks."

Linda stepped up to Lance. "I'd watch my back if I were you," she told him looking right at me.

He looked at me and I shrugged.

"Okay, Linda. Take care." He told her, smiling.

She got into the passenger side of the truck. Vinnie started it and waved to Lance before driving away. Lance came up and searched my face to make sure I was all right. He turned me around, put an arm around my shoulder and took me inside.

"Whoa," he said when he finally saw it.

Only thing missing after that haul-away was an echo. I sat on the edge of the cot and Lance sat next to me.

The sun was going down and a light breeze blew in on us through the opened front door.

"Feel like a camp out?" he asked.

Lance went home and came back with his camping gear. We opened all the windows in the cottage so it would be cold and smell like the outdoors. Then we pitched the tent in the bedroom. We lit it with a battery-powered camping lamp and shared a pot of tea.

"Do you think it's possible to know someone else?" I asked, handing Lance a cup of tea.

"Possible, but not likely. Look what goes into it, quantity, duration, right circumstances."

"Then how do you measure a friendship?"

"By how familiar I am with someone," he said with a smile.

"What if you're not familiar with someone but they do everything you think a true friend would do?"

"Then I know by whether her pupils dilate when she looks at me."

"Seriously, Lance."

"I don't think about it, Tulsa. Thinking about it defeats the purpose of trying to know someone else."

"So you do think it's possible?"

"Possible, but not likely."

"What if it happens? What then?"

"You grow bored. Everybody grows bored. Human beings require novelty or thy wander."

"How grim."

"Happy endings are a fabrication to inspire courage in children. Life is filled with unwanted indignities and bitter disappointments. Must indoctrinate the peasants so they will toil away their lives."

"Indignities and bitter disappointments?"

"Enough. Like the indignity of never seeing my parents while growing up except during the occasional formal dinners for prominent guests."

"Prominent guests?"

"I have an idea how to save the situation. But I might have to crash here. On the cot?"

"What?"

"I will take care of it. Can I crash here? I brought music." Lance leaned back on the pad and sleeping bag he had put out for me. "If this is uncomfortable, you can put the cot in here," he said, smiling.

"Why would you move out of your place? I thought it was yours."

"I can't go there. My situation has changed."

11

The next morning I heard the Lance rap and thought it was the front door. I went out of the tent to go and answer. The front room was empty. I heard the knocking again as I opened the front door. There was no one there. Then I saw Lance at the landlady's backdoor. I watched while the door opened and he talked to someone I assumed was the landlady but I couldn't hear what they said. After a few minutes they went inside. That surprised me but I assumed he would be right back out for me so I could join them in the discussion.

I waited there expectantly watching the landlady's door for longer than comfortable and finally went inside. I went straight away to put the kettle on for tea. An hour later, Lance came into the cottage smiling. "She said since Linda didn't give notice, her deposit can be ours."

"She doesn't want to meet me?"

"She's all right with it. I made a deal to help her out around here, collecting rent, overseeing repairs, whatever she needs."

"What do you know about repairs?"

Lance chuckled.

He moved his few things in that afternoon, one of which was a manual typewriter.

"Mind if I use it sometime?"

"Anytime."

"How about now?"

Lance dug out a ream of paper and set me up with the typewriter on an upside down crate. He put one of his pillows on the floor for me to sit on.

I had to write a letter to Hector's supervisor. I had found that name with a few phone calls to human resources and I was going to write to whichever agency took reports of sexual harassment. I planned on making copies and taking them in to show Hector that night, but when I found out the "i" didn't work, I had to type the letters at the library.

The next night, Lance escorted me to the Beef Corral when it was just about to close and we sat down in a booth. Linda took our drink order. She kept glancing at Lance. She was a little stiff and formal at first but Lance's smile melted her in no time. She paid scant attention to me. I watched her go nervously into the back after she had given us our drinks. When Linda came out I signaled her over.

"Please tell Hector I'm here."

Linda glanced at Lance. "Listen," she said to me, "you think you know what's going on but you don't. Just mind your own business." She put our check down on the table. "Thanks, and have a good night," she said, smiling at Lance before walking away.

"What's going on?" Lance asked me, amused.

"I have to go talk to the manager. I'll be right back."

I walked to the back keeping a tight-fisted hold on the envelopes. I opened Hector's door without knocking and ducked in. Hector looked up from his desk and watched me lock the door. He leaned back and put his hands behind his head.

"Hector."

"You're no longer an employee here. I can have the police remove you. Unless you are here as an independent contractor," he suggested helpfully while opening his belt.

"Cool your jets, Romeo," I said, fanning out the envelopes and holding them up in front of his face. "You don't want your life to be turned upside down, right? How would that go over with your family?"

Hector grabbed the envelopes and yanked out the letters. He read through them then tore them up.

"Hey, be glad it's me and not some idiot who would wreck everything for everybody. Think, Hector. I have copies."

He charged at me, and I thought here comes a beating. I backed against the door and unlocked it. He shoved me aside and locked it. "Sit down," he commanded.

I sat down.

He stood by the door, looking down at me. "If you do anything, I will make sure you are very sorry," he told me. I stood and walked up to him, smiling as sweetly as I was able and winked."

"Wouldn't it be better to just go on without being bothered and pay me my regular salary in weekly installments? Everybody stays happy." I was so close, I was breathing on him.

"Better if you came in once a week after hours to earn it," he said smiling, almost under my spell.

"But that is not the offer, Hector. You have ten seconds to decide."

"How about if I gave you some pleasure?"

"Six seconds," I said, feeling truly ill at the thought. "I expect the first money order in the mail in two days or your degenerate life will be a lot more stressful," I told him, still smiling and opening the door to go out. I stopped and closed the door again.

"Um, how about an advance? I'm desperate. I'm likely to do any crazy thing, backed in a corner like this."

He opened his wallet and gave me what he had.

Linda gave me an evil look when I passed her on my way to Lance who was standing by the booth. I smiled at him. He always seemed formal despite every effort to appear casual. He took me by the elbow and opened the door for me to go out. He didn't look back at Linda who stood there, hands indignantly on her hips, wearing that ridiculous uniform.

That night, Lance and I hung out in the tent.

"Are you going to tell me what's going on at your job?"

"It's not my job, I don't work there anymore. But don't worry about whether I can pay the bills," I said, handing him a stack of cash. "That should cover me to next month."

"What happened?"

"Linda."

"What did she mean when she said you think you know what's going on?"

"Just workplace drama, Lance. Goes on everywhere. You wouldn't know since you never worked and never will. There's nothing but drama in the workplace, believe me."

"Okay, Tulsa, what else is up with you?"

"Tell me why you moved in here with me."

"My father cut me off. What about you?"

"It really was the Linda thing at work."

Lance leaned over and whispered in my ear. "I'm not the enemy."

I felt suddenly icy cold and violently shivered. Lance pulled the blanket over my shoulders to cover me. It felt awkward and I was uncertain how to react or position myself. He poured me tea and put it in my hands. I sipped it and watched him. He was studying my hair, my nose, my hands, my neck, my lips and my eyes. He set my tea aside and kissed me.

I had wondered what that would feel like. Every time I had been with a guy making out I had hoped for what I was feeling when Lance kissed me.

Lance left late mornings to "take care of business," and I didn't find out until later that meant schmoozing with his dad and buddies at the country club. Then Lance gradually started spending an hour here or there in the landlady's house.

"What's she like?" I asked him one day after he had been in there for an hour and a half.

"In very good shape for her age."

"What do you mean shape? Her body?"

He chuckled.

"What do you talk to her about?"

"Why? Are you jealous?"

"Curious."

"You are jealous."

"God, I hope not." I thought of Linda.

He gave me a quick kiss and went to the bathroom to take a shower.

I followed him and leaned in the doorway.

"How old is she?"

"I don't know, fifty, maybe," he said adjusting the water temperature.

"Do you like her?"

"Like her? How do you mean?" he asked, undressing and smiling at me.

I couldn't help smiling, too. He was gorgeous. "What, Lance?

"You mean the way I like you?" he asked, referring to his erection.

"Something like that."

"No, it's business with her," he told me while going behind the shower curtain. The curtain was clear plastic with a jungle motif.

"What is it with me, Lance?"

"Pleasure, obviously."

"Why is what you do there such a secret?"

"Why is what happened at your job a secret?"

"I might tell if you tell me what you do with that woman for hours."

He reached out for me. I went over and let him drape his wet arm around me. He kissed my neck, my cheeks, and my eyes.

"Where are you going?" I asked, fighting the tranquilizing almost incapacitating effect of his kisses.

"My father's."

"His house?" It wasn't feeling right, not one bit.

"Finally."

"Great."

The next morning I opened the door to look out while I sipped my tea. It was overcast and gloomy. It struck me as rather strange at first because the weather had been nothing but sunny for weeks but I shrugged it off. As I turned to go back inside, a crow screamed at me. I looked back and saw it sitting there in a branch over the landlady's house. It looked at me and cackled. "Very funny," I said and turned to go in and sit down. The crow made a dive at the door of the cottage letting out a shriek. I almost dropped the tea. I had to steady myself with one hand while I sat the saucer and cup down. I looked out and saw the crow there in the tree, looking down at me. Then it took wing and left. Just like that.

That was about the same time the terrible burden of memories, that edgy sense of impending doom and my perpetual secret typing began.

I never saw a crow in all the time I lived there except that one. And it made me yearn to be in the canyon and taunted by those rowdy crows up there. So I made a trip back. First time since I was a kid. The canyon was dry and the hike up hot and dusty. There were no people and mostly flies. Mudslides must have changed things. There was no sense in going further to see the pool or those tiny frogs. It was like they had never been there.

It only follows that I would next search for immersion by crowd swallow at a rave. I went through the crowd and they all seemed to move away from me and closer to one another. I saw her again, Daria, looking out over the heads around her. She wore a tiara and white gown and appeared to be searching the room for someone. My chest constricted and I felt scared and excited at the same time. I heard a minion call to her, "Daria!" She waved back and made her way over to kiss this admirer. Then off again she went to the stage.

I leaned against the wall to watch Daria play the tortured soul at the microphone.

I haven't mastered anything. If this is how we are measured I'm in trouble. I thought I understood people or at least could predict behavior but that's just a lot of crap. People are unpredictable. I haven't mastered anything because I've been living in a kind of floating world. I was never alone or afraid. At least, that was what I was supposed to believe. I was never desperate for company or worried about whose company I was keeping. I floated through places, people's lives, events, eras.

The laughter of others behind closed doors and their secret lives had always been a mystery to me. As the years went on and I faced more closed doors and built nothing for myself, I began to feel sad for the person I was becoming, for an entire life of the same thing forming and spreading out before me. Without my abuela's spirit, there was no protection against fear or a broken heart.

12

I watched through the front window for Lance to emerge from the landlady's closed back door. This must have been how you felt, abuela, each time you waited on the other side of Pop's studio door for his art model to dress and leave. I understood why Concepción died of a broken heart. And I believed that was the reason she watched over me. To make sure I never did.

"Why did you leave, abuela?" I asked out loud.

When Lance appeared, I ducked away from the window and ran into the bathroom, quietly closed the door and locked it. Lance came into the cottage and went straight away to the bathroom, as was his routine after being with her. He always showered.

He tried the doorknob. "Tulsa, you almost done?"

"Almost," I said and flushed the toilet for effect. I turned on the faucet and watched the water splash into the sink then turned it off and unlocked the door. I waited for him to open it because I didn't feel he deserved any courtesies from me.

He opened the door and walked past me. I watched him from the doorway while he undressed. He was sweaty and red faced.

"Want to watch me shower, huh?" he said, putting on that smile.

"Why are you so sweaty?"

"I was working," he slowly slid his shorts off trying to get a reaction.

"Who were you working on?"

Lance smiled. "You are jealous," he said, turning on the shower.

I glanced at myself in the mirror. I appeared more worried than I wanted to let on so I allowed my features to soften. Lance took the opportunity when my back was to him to hop in the shower. But I could see him in the mirror and the even rows of bright red welts on the back of his thighs.

He poked his head out from the shower curtain. "Will you believe me if I said you have nothing to worry about with her?"

"I'm not worried, do I look worried to you?" I asked and checked myself in the mirror. "I'm just curious. What work are you doing over there?"

Lance went back under the shower. Damn, I thought, I sound clingy.

"Come here," he said, opening the curtain and leaning out. I let him pull me into the shower, into his arms under the water. I wanted to tell him about my arrangement with Hector, but it would be like exposing the soft underbelly of my life so he could more easily rip it open.

"You mean a lot to me," he told me with such intimate sincerity I wanted to believe him.

"Okay," I said to please him.

"I have to take off. How about I bring food later?" he asked then released me to go back to his shower.

I backed away, dripping wet in my droopy soaked clothes, and asked pathetically, "Where are you going?"

"I have a lunch appointment with my father."

I left the room.

While Lance got dressed in his meeting-father-attire, I read in the tent. He shouted goodbye on his way out. I was alone again, still wet from his embrace in the shower, now cold, but the inertia of disappointment and creeping heartbreak prevented me from moving let alone changing my wet clothes. I grew angrier at Lance and proportionately chilled throughout the night.

I woke up the next morning weak and sore. I went into the front room hoping to find Lance or a clue he had been there. Nothing. I changed into warmer clothes and went back to bed. I slept most of the day, on occasion waking to read in a fever induced stupor. After dark, I got up to lock the front door and turn on the porch light.

Weak and exhausted, I dropped into the stuffed chair with a crackling of papers under the cushion. I thought maybe I had better be more careful when I stash my pages. There were too many to conceal. I pulled the stack out and straightened them. I read here and there stories about Pops. My throat constricted. Pops had been all I had in life. I had never tried to see him again and whenever I thought of him, I always imagined him in the same place. It dawned on me that he was an old man and I was overcome with a terrible sadness. If I lost him it would be a deeper loss than my abuela's spirit, far more dismal. If Pops were to die, my only connection to another human being in this world died with him. A violent shiver shook me suddenly. I put the pages back under the cushion and went back to bed.

By morning, I was shivering with fever. I dragged myself out of bed, pulled on winter socks and shoes, a jacket over the clothes I had slept in, and I left the cottage with only a few bills and some change in my pocket. It was one block to the bus stop. Three hours and two buses later, I got off in front of a gas station and walked to The Arms apartments in a feverish haze.

There were townhouses where the aircraft junk yard used to be. The apartment building itself was the same. At the security entrance, I buzzed a random apartment. Only then did I wonder why I was there. What was I expecting?

"Yes?" a man asked from the intercom.

"Hi, uh, I'm here to meet my grandfather but he's not here yet. I need someone to let me in."

The door buzzed and I stepped into the courtyard. It was quiet. Nobody was around. I gripped the hand-rail and climbed the stairs towards Pops' apartment. I noticed the pool was empty. I thought I heard a crow at that moment but if I did, I couldn't see where.

It frightened me to realize I would be seeing Pops again. I told myself there was nothing to be afraid of and when I reached the top of the stairs I noticed the yellow tape across his door and window. Fear gripped my chest and lifted the hair on my arms.

"No," I said and went over.

Crime scene.

I tore the tape away and threw it over the banister. The door was locked. I slid down against it, put my face in my hands and sat there sobbing, oblivious to every-thing except my grief. When the sobs slowed down, I remembered where I was and looked up at Blanche's door. I pulled myself up, wiped my face on my sleeve, and headed over there. I knocked and waited with my head down. A woman I didn't know answered.

"Can I help you?" she tentatively asked.

"Is Blanche here?" I glanced in at the unfamiliar furniture behind her.

"I'm sorry, I don't know who that is," she said and closed the door a bit to bar my view of her place.

"Thanks," I said in a small voice and turned away.

"Can I help?" she called after me.

I stopped with my back to her and realized I had to find out.

"Yes," I said. "What happened over there?" I pointed at Pops' door.

"Didn't you see it in the news?"

"In the news?"

"Burglary, homicide. Terrible tragedy. Nice old guy. An artist. Did you know him?"

"Better than anyone," I said in a daze and turned to go.

13

During the bus ride back, I was barely conscious. I took brief note when I arrived that Lance was still not there. Then I changed into layers of warm clothes and got into the sleeping bag in the tent.

Sometime during the night, the front door slammed shut and startled me awake. My head throbbed and I was sore all over. I heard heavy footsteps and Lance's voice.

A wave of dizziness came over me and I closed my eyes.

I was suddenly in a small boat surrounded by vast blue water. Rolling waves gently rocked me. From far off, I heard a familiar singing.

"The other night dear, as I lay sleeping, I dreamt I held you in my arms. But when I woke, dear, I was mistaken, so I hung down my head and I cried."

There was nothing around but infinite blue stillness.

I looked over the side of the boat. Reflected in the water from a source I could not see, were Pops and Concepción next to me in the boat. They smiled at me. I looked around but I was alone until I looked back at the water. Concepción was no longer a child. She was in her mid-thirties, slim and beautiful. She wore an adult version of the quinceañera dress that she had worn in the photograph of herself at fifteen. It was the same dress she was wearing in her visitations. Pops looked very old, but he still had that same mischievous sparkle in his eyes. He winked at me. Concepción draped her arms around Pops, gave him a squeeze and looked at me as if to show me how glad she was to be with him.

"Tulsa?" It sounded so near, I looked behind me in the empty boat.

I turned back to the water, but they were no longer there. The sky darkened. The water was suddenly rough around the boat and rapidly became violent. A wave crashed down and cast me out right before smashing the boat apart. I was thrown into the water and slipped beneath its surface. I plummeted downward into the deepest ocean, pulled under by Moby Dick and an awful curse of fate.

"Tulsa?" it came again, muffled and far off. "We have to bring your fever down. Help me."

I kicked and fought Lance while he undressed me. After stripping me naked, he took my clothes out of the tent and returned with a bottle of alcohol.

"Help me, Tulsa! We have to bring your fever down," he demanded and splashed alcohol on my feet and up my legs. I screamed from the burning pain it caused and tried kicking him away but I didn't have the strength. I drifted in and out of consciousness while Lance tortured me with occasional alcohol rubs. It hurt less each time and finally felt soothing. I relaxed enough at last to let him tend to me without squirming.

I eventually looked at Lance who sat with my head in his lap. He saw that I was with him and capped the alcohol. He helped me into the sleeping bag and zipped it up.

Lance sat next to me and wiped wet strands of hair out of my face.

"You had me scared for a minute there, Tulsa."

"Scared?"

Lance looked down.

Then it hit me that I might have been in serious danger and Lance just saved my life. I couldn't figure out if he was relieved to avoid the personal distress of having to call the authorities and deal with a dead body or actually feared losing me.

"What were you doing to my feet?"

"I had to, Tulsa, to bring your temperature down as soon as possible."

"Where'd you learn to do that?"

"Au pair in Bora Bora. She had to do it once when my parents took us along on a vacation. They left us alone in the hotel while they went out on the yacht without any way to contact them. Au pair was covered with bruises from it. I fought like hell to avoid being naked in front of her. If she saw me naked, she would find out my little secret. I was tormented by constant erections from the moment I saw her. Even in that feverish state. Mortified. The delirium spared me no shame."

"How old were you?"

"I was fourteen. She was twenty-eight." Lance closed his eyes and shook his head.

"That doesn't sound right."

"Don't worry. She loved me like a brother."

"How would you know? You're an only child."

"I meant it euphemistically."

"She had sex with you?"

"No, but I've been having sex with her ever since. Until you, of course. And now I am going to make sure you're on your feet in no time."

That's exactly what he did. He fed me chicken noodle soup from scratch, fed me oranges, and tried to drown me in pitcher after pitcher of water. I pretended to feel sick after I was well enough to leave the bed. There was comfort in Lance's attentions. It relaxed me enough to sleep and allowed dreams to deliver me from reflection.

Lance got me on my feet, but as soon as I was upright, he went back to spending time with his father and the landlady.

I was determined to find out exactly what was going on between Lance and the landlady and decided what I needed to do. It was the only way to get a hold of the situation.

I kept track of his every move without letting on. I watched closely through the cottage windows as lights came on in the landlady's house and noted the rooms they spent their time in. When Lance went inside, a light on the second floor soon came on and went off always around an hour and twenty minutes later, moments before he came back out.

I finally had all I needed to know to sneak over there one night. The room they occupied opened onto a terrace that could be accessed from an outside staircase. Ducking in the shadows under the terrace, I listened. I thought I heard something, maybe a voice, but I wasn't sure.

While I climbed the stairs I heard something again, definitely a woman's voice. Once I reached the top step,

I could hear better but not what she was saying. I inched toward the French doors to find out. The curtains were parted slightly and revealed a strip of light. The outside light was off so I knew I could see in without being seen. I moved in closer and peered in at the narrow view of the room.

I was startled to see that the room was entirely red. There was a fainting couch to one side. A woman sat on it in a black latex mini skirt, her legs bare. She wore six-inch spiked heels. I couldn't see her above the hips.

"Over here," I heard her say.

I looked around at what I could see of the room. On one side was a gold-framed antique mirror that was almost as high as the ten foot ceiling. Nearby sat what appeared to be a padded sawhorse with built in steel rings. On the opposite wall hung a horsehair whip, black leather riding crop, a black leather paddle, a smooth wood paddle, padded wrist cuffs, and latex mask equipped with a gag. Lance came into view as he crossed the room. Naked.

"On your knees," she commanded. He kept his hands crossed at his back while he knelt down.

I jolted back and the boards creaked under me. I went as quickly and silently as I could down the steps and straight into the cottage. I ran in to watch through the window.

The light on the terrace went on but no one came out. I watched until I was too tired to stand there waiting for who knows what, then I went in the tent to sleep.

The cottage front door banged shut and I heard Lance breeze through on the way to the obligatory shower. I imagined myself microscopically small and under his radar. I thought I might be spared having to face him. But there he appeared, at the opening of the tent.

"May I come in?" he asked, coming in.

"Linda was right about one thing," he said, baiting me. "You think you know what's going on but you don't."

"Lance," I asked, "why are you here? Living here, I mean."

"You want me to move?"

"I'm just wondering."

"You want me to go?" he asked again, standing.

"You know I can't afford to live here alone."

"Look, Tulsa, I have a situation and I'm doing what I can to take care of it. I can't move right now either. You need to back off a little."

"You need to stop coming to my bed."

"If that's what you want," he said, and left the room.

For a moment I was stunned by his tone. Then I was pissed that he had ever kissed me in the first place. I charged out of the tent and into the front room. Lance was lying on the cot. He put his hand up to stop me from speaking before I opened my mouth. I went right on in to the kitchen and put the kettle on. I ignored him on my way through to the bedroom and slammed the door for emphasis.

Once in the tent, I broke down and silently cried into my tea, forgetting to sip it until it was too cold and bitter to enjoy.

Later I shook off the shroud of self-pity and thought seriously about my situation for the first time. I tried to maintain an attitude of moral self-righteousness about the goings on in the red room but kept coming back to my arrangement with Hector. I had no way of knowing whether what Lance did over there was legal or not. If I were caught, I'd surely go to jail. If he was caught, at this point, he might only be embarrassed. Would serve him right, though. And Hector deserved what he got. He was a bad person.

Then I thought of the women at The Beef Corral degrading themselves. They did it of their own free will but I knew they felt forced by poverty and limited options. Some had children. A few where in trade school to better their lives. Some were bitches and basically unpleasant human beings but I guess they felt they had more to lose by giving up their jobs than I did. I had nothing going in.

But I didn't like any of it, Hector, Lance or the landlady. I wanted to be done with all of it.

Whatever I decided, I was going to need money.

Looked like there was only one thing to do.

Rent money in hand, I rode a bus to the local mega-electronics store. Once there, I wandered for a while in a daze until I somehow focused enough to find what I needed and escape further disorientation.

When I opened the door I was startled to see Lance inside on the cot, wearing headphones and reading. I couldn't tell if he noticed my reaction so I continued on in, trying to act natural.

"Where were you?" he asked.

"Right," I said, rolling my eyes on my way with the package to the bedroom. "As if you have a right to ask me anything about what I'm up to," I shut the bedroom door.

The next morning after Lance left, I took the bag out from hiding and stashed it in my traveling case. I dug out the manual and took it into the tent to study. After a while I loaded the film.

The next time Lance returned to the landlady's den of iniquity I was ready.

I didn't have long to wait. Later that night, I heard a car driving up and looked out the window to see who it was. Lance was getting out of a cab. After paying, he walked straight to the landlady's back door. I leapt into to action. I threw on black clothes and grabbed the camera from my case.

Nobody was outside. I weaved my way to the landlady's house, ducking from shadow to shadow and hastening a stealthy climb up the stairs. I was silent in my approach to the French doors. The curtain was parted slightly as before. I lifted the camera and put my eye to the viewfinder to have a look into the room through the lens.

Lance was naked and draped over the padded sawhorse face down with his wrists cuffed and secured to the legs. A tall, statuesque and vogue middle-aged woman, wearing a classic corset and a skin tight shredded raw silk skirt, towered over him, made even taller by a pair of thirties French couture four-inch heels. She was caning the white flesh on his thighs between the marks of previous lashings. She wore a mask. I nearly forgot to take pictures.

The landlady's powerful and graceful movements entranced me. She brought the cane down on Lance's thigh with rapid precision. I imagined the cane whistling as it cut through the air and snapped against his flesh.

Thin red welts blossomed in perfect, even stripes. I imagined tears welling up in his eyes. She stopped and circled the sawhorse.

A picture went through my head of Lance being instructed by a stern governess. My god, I thought, the hired caretakers provided his formative sexual experiences. I lowered the camera and put my eye close to the pane and looked over at the other side of the room. A man in a suit and woman in skirt and heels sat together on the fainting couch, presumably watching. I raised the camera and zoomed in to get a better look. There she was, Daria. She whispered playfully in the man's ear.

A porch light went on in our neighbor's cottage across the courtyard and I ducked, hoping the railing and moonless night would hide me. I crawled over to the stairs and sat at the top. I could see the neighbor's place through the railing and waited to make sure no one came out before hastening a speedy return to the cottage.

Once inside, I immediately hid the camera in the case and the film in the dark recesses behind the cleaning supplies under the kitchen sink, a place Lance didn't even know existed.

I changed my clothes and got into the tent and picked up a random book from my pile. While lying there, I heard a neighbor's door shut. I went out of the tent to spy through the window. The woman next door, who found Lance so amusing whenever he came by to collect her rent, marched dutifully by on her way to the back door of the landlady's house. I ran to the front room to watch. It took quite a while for the landlady to answer.

She was wearing a robe from what I could tell. The neighbor told her something and gestured toward the balcony. The landlady folded her arms and followed the neighbor out far enough to survey the porch and French doors. The neighbor gestured toward her own cottage. The landlady said something. The neighbor shrugged and shook her head. I kept watching after the neighbor left and the landlady went inside.

A few minutes later, the upstairs light went out. Nothing happened for twenty minutes after that. I felt certain they didn't know it was me. When Lance came charging out, it occurred to me he might have guessed. I dashed into the bedroom and to bed. I raised a book to my face just as the front door slammed. Lance charged into the tent, clamped a hand on my wrist and hauled me out.

"What the hell do you think you're doing?" he asked through his teeth.

"Let go!"

"Where is it?" he asked me, a little too rabid a look in his eyes.

"I have no idea what you're talking about."

Lance threw my wrist away in disgust and proceeded to tear apart the cottage. I hovered with my arms folded affecting an affronted attitude. I nearly lost my composure when he found the camera in the case. He looked inside for film. Not finding anything, he threw the camera aside and came after me. I ducked by him and grabbed the camera to see if it was damaged. Lance got a hold of my upper arm and spun me around to face him.

"You're going to tell me where the film is. When they find out, and they will, they're going to think I was involved."

"They?"

"Did you think you would away get with it? My father just got me out of involuntary manslaughter, Tulsa. You think anything is going to happen to me?"

"What?"

"I hit a car."

"You killed someone?"

Lance sat on the cot and put his face in his hands. Was I supposed to feel sorry for him?

"Wait a minute; don't they take away your license when you kill people with your car?"

"You have no idea what you have done," he put his face in his hands and shook his head.

"How do you know the landlady?"

"Tulsa, don't you get it? Course I know her. Everybody knows her."

Lance leapt up and grabbed my arm, too roughly, I thought. "I bruise easily," I told him.

"Then tell me where the film is."

"You're hurting me," I said, looking at his grip on my arm. He removed his fingers revealing red marks.

"You left a stain."

I went into the tent and tucked myself into the sleeping bag.

14

I dozed in fits and was mostly awake throughout the night. When morning came I got up, had my tea, and got dressed. Then, as though it were the natural continuation of my morning routine, I packed Pop's traveling case. I did it on automatic. The pull of the inevitable.

Hours later, I heard a car arrive and looked outside. Lance was parking a convertible 1964 red Mustang. I went to put the kettle on and didn't turn around when I heard him come in.

"Steal a car?" I said, staring absently at the licking blue flames. It became clear at that moment exactly what I had to do. And I had to act fast.

I went into the bedroom to retrieve my backpack and set it by the front door.

"I need a ride."

"A ride? Where?"

"After what you've just done to me, you think you could give me a ride without asking questions? Or even talking much?"

Lance silently picked up the pack and took it out to the car. I got the film out from under the sink and put it along with the typed pages and typewriter in Pops' case and went outside with it. Lance was slumped behind the wheel. I put the case in the back seat. "I left a ring in the bathroom," I told him. "Could you get it for me?"

Lance left the engine running and dragged himself into the cottage. I got into the driver's seat, put the car in gear, and drove out. I felt a pang of regret and almost panic as I sped out of the gravel driveway. Lance ran out of the cottage and after the car. I pulled out onto the street and watched him in the rear-view mirror, running and trying to reach me but quickly receding.

I had planned no further than leaving and found myself mindlessly driving in circles around the neighborhood. There was no leaving, not yet. An umbilical of disappointment-fueled rage held me to Lance. I found a pay phone and called him.

"I still have the film. Just forget about me and let me be on my way."

"You don't understand. You're making a big mistake!" he shouted into the phone.

I hung up.

There, that's it.

I drove back into traffic and headed out. The expanse of the city kept me enveloped for hours without any sign of opening up which I welcomed. The concentration and attention needed kept me from thinking of anything else. So it wasn't thinking that brought me to The Arms apartments, it was a primal inclination, a return to the familiar, like a lost dog sniffing its own trail back to its last home. Or as close to home as it got for this stray dog.

A tenant going in let me into the building. I went up the stairs toward Pops' apartment. The tape was gone and the door was open. I went over and watched the back of a man while he vacuumed in the empty room. When he finished, he switched off the vacuum and unplugged it from the wall. He turned around and was startled to see me.

"What happened to everything that was here?"

"Can I help you?"

"Yes. Can you tell me where all Pops' stuff went?"

"And you are?"

"His granddaughter."

He looked like I'd just told him he won the lottery. "The granddaughter? Thank God you're here!"

He took me to his apartment and sat me in the front room with a glass of water. He dug through stacks of paper on his home-assembled pressboard desk.

"I'm so sorry for your loss," he said while hunting for something he claimed was for me. "I was hoping you'd come, you know, read about it or see it in the news."

He came over and gave me a scrap of paper with an address on it.

"That's where the furniture went. Took it there myself."

"Who's there?"

"It's a public storage. His friend made the arrangements. She told me about you."

Blanche.

I spent the next day in the Mustang parked across the street from the entrance to the storage facility. Just when I was beginning to ripen and reek and would have to leave my surveillance to find a way of cleaning up, a woman pulled into the drive that looked like Blanche. I got out and ran across the street.

But when I caught up with her, I saw that I was obviously wrong. I started to jaywalk to the car and almost got hit by a bus. I hopped back up to the curb and waited in a sleep-deprived stupor while the bus let off a few passengers in front of me. Only after I was back at the Mustang did I notice an older woman standing at the bus stop staring at me. Emotion flooded over me when I realized it was her. Without checking traffic, I ran over and threw myself into her arms.

There I felt warmth and comfort I had not known since Rose sang to me the night she left. Tears ripped out of me and the encompassing pandemonium of the city around us shrank away. We were at that moment all there was to the world. Blanche stroked my dirty hair and rocked me a little.

When I recovered myself she held me at arm's length to have a look at me. She was heavier and her hair was salt and pepper from the gray coming in. But she still possessed her sweetness.

She took me to a storage space and pushed up the corrugated door. Inside were stacks of boxes, some spilling contents into the space, furniture huddled in corners, some of which I recognized as Pops'. A space had been kept clear for a throw rug and two upside down plastic crates. She sat me down on one of them and started digging around in the boxes.

"A week before he died, Pops had me help him write up a will. I joked with him about it, but he said his wife came in a dream and told him they would finally be together."

My throat constricted.

She found some papers and sat with them on the other milk crate.

"We arranged everything. He had already bought plots years ago for all three of you. Pops, Rose and you."

I hung my head. She handed me a folder containing photographs and private investigation reports.

"He's known where Rose is for quite a while. He regretted it, you know. He finally realized the mistakes he made with you. His last paintings were of you."

"How did it happen?"

Blanche handed me a folder of news clippings.

"It's all in there. It was that kid you used to hang out with, Geary? He was robbing Pops and discovered that old Colt .45 under his pillow. There was a struggle and the gun went off. Apparently there was only one bullet. Pops died on the way to the hospital."

I rushed out. Blanche came after me and held my hair out of the way while I vomited on the blacktop outside.

She helped me back in to sit down and dug out a bottle of drinking water for me.

"I put that bullet there" I told her.

"What are you talking about, honey?"

"It's because of me Geary knew about the coins in the first place. I led him there and loaded the pistol."

15

I vaguely remember Blanche tucking me into the bed. I slept for two days in Blanche's bed and when I awoke, I felt rested and strong. But I still felt burdened by what had happened and I hesitated and faltered in every little thing I did. I dropped cups and broke things so I stopped trying to help with dinner or gathering dishes. I was good for washing anything without a sharp edge.

Each day we took care of the shopping or cooking, watched television, and went to bed. No talk about what happened or what I had been doing, just the immediate such as what we planned for dinner and what we needed from the market. We lived this way for a week. By the end of the week I relaxed enough not to be so hazardous.

I started paying more attention to my surroundings and finally noticed more about Blanche's apartment. The only pictures she displayed of Double D were when they were kids. Her possessions were piled in crowded stacks as if the apartment were more of a storage space she slept in.

I noticed Blanche more too, her acerbic disappointment in human nature and obstinate inability to take control of her life. I think she was crippled with heartbreak.

Blanche never mentioned Double D, and she never got a call from either of them in that week. She never received a call from anybody. Over breakfast one day, I asked how they were.

"Oh, well, Denise is in the service and Debbie is in Florida with her family."

"That sounds great, Blanche. Do you have any grandkids?"

Blanche looked down at her plate and shuffled food around.

"I'm sorry," I said, feeling uneasy. "I didn't mean to bring up…"

"Oh, no," she put her hand over mine. "You mustn't doubt yourself so much, Tulsa. I have grandchildren. I wish I had pictures but I don't."

I wondered what could possibly prevent Double D from sending Blanche pictures of her grandkids. I looked around the crowded tiny apartment and wondered what life she was piling up this stuff for. What did she think was coming? It was more like she was barricading herself against awful truths.

"I'm having a hard time with something, maybe you can help me. I think there's a lot of meanness and suffering in the world," I told her, making sure to look her in the eye. "I know you do too. But don't you hope that I will forgive Pops? Right? How do I forgive Pops when my heart is burdened by a world of meanness and suffering? Is forgiveness selective? Do I let him off while holding the rest of humanity to the mat?

"The important thing is not to regret any of it. Leave it where it is. The past you can do nothing about."

I looked at Blanche's neglected past piled around us.

"It crossed my mind one or two times that I could have done more," she confessed, "I could have done more for you. But rewriting the past is a silly distraction from facing the present."

Which she was obviously not doing.

I felt a sweet fondness for Blanche at that moment, for her honest but failed effort to raise daughters who had been born without eyes to see her. I went over and hugged her.

"You're a great mom," I told her. "They don't know what they're missing."

We didn't talk about family matters again until a few days later. Blanche had asked for a ride to storage. I sat on a crate while Blanche went through boxes and told stories related to objects she found. Pops' sofa towered nearby on its side among other pieces of furniture I recognized.

"How come he never got rid of this old stuff?"

"He was miserly. And the state of his furnishings was never a concern to him. He only cared about painting."

"You're telling me," I said with a hint of bitterness.

"And he cared about you and Rose."

"Yes, I have a very caring family."

"He did," she said, smiling, "he loved you."

Then she got up to continue sifting through a crate of papers and files. She pulled out a small, framed painting and handed it to me.

It was a copy of a photograph he had taken of me on my fifteenth birthday. I had forgotten all about that day until then.

Each birthday passed with a cake Pops brought home from the grocery store and a single candle at the top. Every year I blew out that candle wishing for hives behind his knees or boils on his butt or a great big sty in each eye and hairy warts on his face.

On that day I discovered he had written "Feliz quinceañera" on all the chalkboards throughout the apartment. He was in his studio working away on something the night before when I went to bed in a moribund state thinking how sad and lonely another silent birthday was going to be. I had tried to think up a torturous ailment to wish on him for the coming year and considered poison oak rash in his armpits but fell asleep before deciding.

While I ate cold cereal at the table as I had since my first morning there, I allowed myself to imagine it was the day Pops would speak to me once again.

He emerged from the studio disheveled and dark under the eyes and presented a framed picture to me. It was the Polaroid Blanche had taken on the day Rose left. He had it in a handmade wooden frame with intricately carved flourishes at each edge and a sacred heart carved and painted at the top. He lit candles on a cake he had ordered at a fancy bakery with "15" written on top. He took a photograph of me sitting by the lit cake holding the framed Polaroid. When I blew out the candles, I felt sorry about every bad thing I had ever wished on Pops and this time wished for his happiness.

Pops had painted a copy of the photograph three times the original size and framed it. He had painted it only a few months before he was killed.

All the others in the series depicted me without the look of ugly intent on my face while wishing before blowing out the candles. Blanche told me Pops loved me dearly but maybe he was making me more forgiving than he was. I tried to hand back the painting but Blanche wouldn't take it.

"There's a bunch of them like that. *The Birthday Series* he called them. They're around here somewhere. I just have to get organized." Rose went about searching then sat heavily down.

"I helped Pops with the arrangements because I loved him but it was hard after what happened, Tulsa. The phone calls from journalists and TV reporters. I'm sorry his things aren't more organized, but I did my best."

"Pops obviously knew he had a good friend in you."

"I was the first to find him right after it happened. He was still alive. I held his head in my lap while others called the ambulance. We all heard the shot and most of us came out. Geary had already run off. They caught him later. I thought Pops could live through anything. I had no doubt he was going to pull through. He had that sureness up to the end. He made me swear I would find you so you could tell Rose he was gone and recover the painting she took that night she left you with him."

They took him and it was the last I saw him alive. I could hardly believe it was serious. I could not believe he was actually going to leave within a matter of days. I think because it frightened me so much. That awful overlap of life with death like that, it was too intense to even have an exchange about whether I wanted chamomile or black tea. How precious our time is in this world, Tulsa. How sad when it is wasted. If I could go back and change one thing I would have spent as much time needed showing you how precious your life is. Pops was right about one thing, you are the one, at least for me. So go for me. Go tell Rose and get Pops' painting. You're the one.

I slumped forward.

"In those last few weeks, Pops told me a lot." She paused until I looked up at her. "He said he had been granted three perfect chances to know the precious soul of a woman in his wife, daughter, and granddaughter and missed it every time. That, he said, is the irony of his art."

"It's a sham," I corrected. "That isn't irony it's fakery. He's little better than a third rate lewd art photographer."

"Tulsa, I am deeply, deeply sorry I let Pops' silence go on that way."

"Don't worry, Blanche, makes no difference now."

"But it does, it makes all the difference. It cast darkness over your heart for him. And I know I played a part in that. I questioned him about it once. He said there was a thing or two he could tell me about the way I was raising my daughters, did I want to hear? I was terrified of facing what was wrong in my life. I couldn't chance even a hairline crack because instinctively I knew it wouldn't hold. It would all come crashing down."

"I love Pops, I do. It's not all that dark over my heart for him. I just know him. I knew him better than anybody and can bet he wasn't much different when he died from when I last saw him. Pops was Pops. He wasn't made to change. His personality was too large and overdeveloped. I knew Pops better than anybody, believe me."

"Yes, you two were a lot alike. But I think, as much as he loved you and Rose, and loved painting, he loved your grandmother most of all. She was his truest love. The day he asked me to help him with his final preparations, he said Concepción had visited in a dream the night before and reassured him that they would soon be together. It was all that consoled me after the violence of his death. I knew they were together and finally truly happy."

The hairs stood up on my neck. I must've looked stricken because Blanche asked me if I was all right. I broke down crying with my face in my hands. Blanche took a tissue out of her purse and waited patiently. Anger quickly rescued me from sorrow. I accepted the tissue and cleaned up the snot and tears.

Right. So I was left without either one of them, I thought. I felt betrayed by Pops and Concepción and their lovely truest true love together forever in joy after death!

"And what about us, Blanche? Who is waiting for us when we die? Who will make us finally truly happy? Don't we get to be happy?"

Blanche was now the one who looked stricken.

"I'm sorry, I just don't understand why we don't get to be happy. Why weren't you my mother?"

"What do you remember about your mother, anything?"

"I remember she dumped me."

"I think your mother loved you and made the biggest mistake of her life and has probably never forgiven herself for it."

"Not a good enough excuse for staying away for a lifetime. You admit you blew it and you try harder. Pops did the same thing, made a mistake not speaking to me and lived his life making the same mistake day after day. You think I'm going to feel sympathy for her mistaken life?"

"You don't have to. Just do your duty to Pops and tell her and get the painting, that's all. It can be very formal and business like."

"My duty to Pops? Are you kidding?"

"He willed his collection to you, Tulsa, on that condition," she said and handed me Pops' last will and testament.

16

She's the one. Oh, brother, I thought. That man put on a good show. Every moment of every day of his life Pops put on a good show. And he's still doing it from beyond the grave. He got it wrong about me though. Yeah, I'm the one. I'm the one to turn the whole thing into cash. They both got it wrong.

I found a small dealer of decorative art who catered to a chic clientele and arranged to show him Pops' work. I brought Pops' last year of paintings, all duplicated from those photographs he took of me every birthday when I was blowing out the candle on my cake and wishing for some torturous ailment on him. In every one he altered the emotional timbre of my gaze into the lens. The idea of turning his twelve little self-delusions into some easy money occurred to me when Blanche found the photographs themselves in storage and proudly gave them to me as if to hand over more evidence of his love.

I showed the dealer some of Pops' nudes to give him the idea of the sort of work Pops did, drive the price of *The Birthday Series* up. He suggested that a good story about this artist could lend interest.

Well, I thought, if it's a good story he wants, I told him "Pops was an outlaw who had robbed twelve liquor stores over the course of his lifetime but he was mostly always painting when he wasn't doing time. He was tall and dark and would have been a notorious lover had irritating skin conditions not plagued him. He was handsome and charismatic and easily convinced women he could ravage them and that is why they bared themselves so brazenly in painting after painting throughout his life."

"Are the nudes available?"

"Not at the moment. Only the twelve I brought are available now. But I'll let you have first offer on the others."

I had not wanted to admit it to myself before but I wasn't a hundred percent sure I had a legal right to sell his work. I sold them anyway. The dealer even agreed to obligate the buyers to loaning out the work when shown. Thought I'd throw that into the negotiations to lend a punctuating legitimacy. I had no plans to find Rose or collect anything for Pops. If his work was ever going to be shown, someone else would have to do the collecting and showing. I'm just putting together the money I will need for the plan for my life I had yet to formulate. That's all I'm here to do, I told myself. I was still seething with wounded pride over Concepción and Pops' death defying loyalty and Blanche's collusion.

When I had asked Blanche if I could have all of Pops' paintings of me over the last year, she spent a few days digging through the stuff in the storage space, moving things around, telling endless meandering stories that were leaden with minutia and handing the paintings over as she recovered them.

Didn't ask me why I wanted them. Didn't ask me why I wanted to borrow two nudes for a day. I kept asking for everything with a conspiratorial smile as if I had great plans and I told her it would be a surprise. I didn't say shock, or profound disappointment. I said surprise. She had implicit trust in me.

She would never think of me as betraying her in any way. To her I was goodness. That was Blanche's downfall; she lived in a world of bright and lovely goodness versus those who have gone astray. She would never imagine deceit coming from me. She couldn't admit I had gone astray because then she'd have to admit she helped me along. And that was her downfall. She could not face that every choice and decision she made created the life she lived. Any admission of responsibility could be the crack that finished her off.

When I came home with that money in my pocket, feeling the pressure of it against the front of my thigh, I could not keep the grin off my face. I didn't have to blackmail anybody for it, I thought, sopping with pride. Blanche had a close look at me, sitting across from her at the kitchen table, grinning, arm draped across the back of the chair.

"You look like the cat that ate the canary."

"If anyone ever asks, Pops was tall, dark and sexy though plagued by irritating skin conditions," I said, chuckling and pulling out the wad of cash. I waved it in all good humor.

Blanche must have had a pretty good idea what I had done.

"Tulsa, you're not about to drag that man's name through the mud, are you?"

"Nothing like that. I'm going to get people to love him no matter what I say he's done. Kind of the way I had to love him."

She looked stricken again.

"It doesn't matter if Pops was ten feet tall," I implored her to follow me. "Or if he was master of the universe. The beauty of what he did is in the honesty of his work." I had Blanche's attention and felt a prickling guilt.

"Pops documented what a fool he remained his entire life with great skill and embarrassing honesty, Blanche."

"He told me," Blanche interrupted, "that painting of Concepción had drained him so much he was bed ridden with a perpetual cough and ear ache for a month after he finished. While he coughed the night away alone in the studio, Concepción nursed Rose and Pops felt distant from them. He said there was a sublime bond between the two. He said their relationship was uncanny and became downright eerie when they began lighting candles and praying at altars of the virgin and saints. He suspected Concepción of teaching Rose a little Santeria. He said you were all cursed with fire and sight."

"If you're trying to get me to think differently about Pops, it's not working. That's all a bunch of crap. The only strain for him painting her was pushing himself past that lazy, superficial representation he always rested on."

"Okay, then you should know that Rose saved money every year to pay an investigator to keep her up to date regarding your whereabouts. She watched your life from a distance in still photographs, sometimes video. That has been her Christmas present to herself all these years and why she lives the way she does."

"Are you kidding me? That's weird and possibly illegal. It only confirms I come from a long line of lunatics and that's like a disclaimer for me. I can be the biggest asshole in the world and I only need to pull out the fucked up family card to excuse my behavior. On the other hand, any sane accomplishment is cause for celebration since the bar is low for me."

Blanche suddenly stood. "They're closing soon."

"How did you know that about Rose?" I asked her.

"I spoke to her on the phone. I never said anything about Pops except that I was his neighbor and I asked if she knew your whereabouts. She knew what happened to him from TV news and had been wondering when she would be contacted. I told her it won't be long."

"Was she trying to get you to feel sorry for her?"

"We better go. This place closes soon."

"Blanche, I loved Pops and I love you. Whatever else, will you try to remember that? It might make you feel better whenever you think of me. Okay?"

"Fine," she said in a small voice.

"I'm not commanding you, you can say no."

"I'll try to remember that you said you love Pops and me."

"Not that I say I do, that I actually do."

"We should probably go. This place is going to close."

"Blanche, that I do, not that I say I do."

"You do, you say you do. All just words anyway, right?"

She was right. They were a lot of words. There was some kind of twisted wisdom in living without words I had to admit. There was more honesty because you don't say one thing and do another. You just did things, no excuses and no explanations.

It was time to head out.

But I felt guilty leaving Blanche high and dry so I swore to her I would carry-out Pops' last wish. What else was I going to say to make sure she cried over my leaving? I tried to sound as sincere as possible because I didn't want Blanche to feel any doubt so she'd like me and be sad to see me leave. Worked out perfectly. She cried. No one had ever cried when I left before.

Once I left I went ahead and filled the gas tank and headed out onto the interstate. Next exit I was off the interstate. I pulled aside and banged my forehead against the steering wheel. There was something I had to take care of before leaving town.

17

I had at first headed out feeling elated but the thought of Hector's wife invaded my reverie. I knew there would be no peace for me, that I would never be able to claim Blanche's tears for my own, if I left things the way they were. I didn't understand how I knew or what came over me but I turned that car around and headed back.

Soon I was in full traffic on the freeway and it wasn't long before I had arrived. I parked across the street. The front door was open but a dark screen door prevented a view inside. This meant, I realized, that whoever is inside could see out. I faced forward, imagining Hector's wife in there watching me.

I wondered if she ever went out. Did Hector ever take her out? I felt like his co-conspirator. I wondered if for her it was better not to know what he was doing and continue living that way, or to know and have your life turned upside down? Which was better? Right now, in her ignorance, she has a home, a complete family, security, hope, a future of grandchildren and holiday dinners.

If she knew? Possibly divorce, restraining orders, loss of financial and housing security. I realized it was not up to me but then I could just come clean and leave the rest up to her. She could always choose to pretend she didn't know. Then they both could settle down in their lies and live unhappily ever after. I calculated how much extortion money I had collected. It was a lot, but I had plenty more than that from the money I got from Pops' paintings.

I took out my wallet and counted out a few thousand in hundreds and put them in my pocket. I left the Mustang and headed over to Hector's front door. I knew Hector would be home from work any minute so I wanted to make it quick. I knocked on the door and shaded my eyes to see in through the screen.

"Hello?" I called.

I thought I could see someone inside. "Hello?"

"May I help you?" I heard the whisper from inside.

"Are you Hector's wife?"

I heard sniffling and ice clinking in a glass. "Who's asking?"

I held up the money. "I want to make sure I give this to the right person."

She came up in a robe, holding a drink, and opened the screen door for me to go inside. She was pretty, maybe late twenties, a cute figure. But she was too hag-gard for her age.

I put the money in her hand. "I can tell you where this money is coming from or it can keep coming, no questions asked. You can put it in an account for you and the kids. It's up to you."

She held up the money.

"That's all I can tell you. You have to decide quickly."

Catching the need for urgency, she retrieved a plastic bag from the kitchen to put the money in.

"I knew there was something," she said, hiding the bag of money under the newspaper lining the birdcage.

I floated back to the car. I felt like the grand prize winner. I drove off puffed up, my arm resting in the win-dow, top down, one hand on the steering wheel, radio loud. I told myself that it must have made up for the wrong toward Blanche.

That got me two off-ramps further than the last time I tried leaving town. I pulled off and parked under a walnut tree. I realized it from the cracking and popping under the tires. I got out of the car and slipped on the walnuts. I landed on my butt and sat there poked and stuck by the broken shells.

I got up pulling pieces from my body and gingerly stepped back to the car. I put the top up and got in but suddenly open the door to vomit in the street. I sat a moment without volition. I could barely lift my arm to check out my reflection in the rear-view mirror. I looked more haggard than Hector's wife.

And I was doing it to myself. If our every choice and decision resulted in the life we live then I put myself right where I was. It was quite an epiphany for me. Quite profound. I had a breakthrough how I could get my pretty back and keep it. I wasn't completely clear on the how, but I did have a sense that certain roads are rougher on one's looks than others. I'm no philosopher but at that moment I was thinking it was best to take care of any unfinished business. Leave clean, stay pretty.

With that in mind, I pulled over at the next thrift store and slept the last few hours before dawn in the back seat of the Mustang. I was wiped out and slept well past sunrise. It was the loud clanging of the thrift store's security gate being slid open that woke me. The woman kept glancing at me nervously. I didn't care. I was all business and it wasn't long before I left that shop wearing a snug fitting red cocktail dress and pumps.

I went straight away to a gas station bathroom and washed my hair then applied red lipstick. Now I was ready to head out.

I checked the address and directions for Rose and headed out onto the highway.

18

For a while I sat there in the lot looking at the building she lived in. There was one row of ground floor rooms, a staircase at both ends leading to a second story with a narrow walkway and metal railing. It was a motel. Rose was living in a cheap motel. I remembered what Blanche said about Rose spending her savings every year on the P.I. to collect pictures and information on me.

Didn't care. Didn't soften my resolve one bit. Still all business. I went to her door and knocked. Rose answered and went right back in but left the door ajar for me to come in. I walked away and could hear the door being slammed shut behind me. I stopped and took a deep breath. I'm here on business. I have to put my personal feelings aside, I told myself. I don't even know this person. She's basically a stranger to me. In this way I strengthened my conviction to go back and knock again. This time Rose held the door open and stepped aside so I could go in.

"Rose, I'm here for the painting. Hand it over and I can go," I said, remaining near the door.

Rose grabbed two beers out of the mini-fridge and gave me one.

"Relax, kid," Rose suggested then went in and leaned against the dresser to drink her beer and check me out.

I had to wade through packages, gifts and old bouquets of flowers to get to the bed and sit on the edge. I put the beer against my forehead.

"Kid. You sound like Pops. Oh yeah, Pops is dead. I killed him."

Rose sat down.

Meanwhile, Lance was outside trying the doors and peering through the windows of the Mustang. Confident he was in the right place, Lance paid the driver of a waiting taxi. The driver took Lance's pack out from the trunk and gave it to him then left.

Totally unaware of Lance's arrival, I continued, "I wasn't the one who pulled the trigger but I loaded that bullet and showed the killer where to find the gun."

"Forget about guilt, kid. It'll wreck your complexion."

"Right, you're probably an expert on that. Your skin looks pretty good."

"So Pops bad-mouthed me?"

"No, he never did."

"What's with the attitude?"

"Are you kidding?"

"You're an adult. Can't still be blaming childhood or me for your woes. You don't get to past eighteen. What are you so bitter about, anyway? Didn't you always have everything you needed? Maybe I couldn't provide all that for you myself but I made damn sure that's how it was going to be. I did what was within my power to be sure you would be safe and well looked after. And were you?"

"Not exactly."

"What? He didn't hurt you, did he?"

"No. He didn't speak to me."

"What do you mean?"

For years Pops would not speak to me. He wrote little notes on chalkboards.

"Years?"

"He spoke to others all the time but refused to speak to me after he was accidentally shot in the foot. By me."

"I'm confused. Does that have anything to do with the recent shooting?"

"Same pistol. Remember from abuela Concepción? I loaded two bullets. Unintentionally shot Pops in the foot with one. He kept that gun with that second bullet all these years. Then the kid I hung out with who got those bullets for me ends up strung out on meth and looks for the family coins and that pistol at Pops' place. Pops caught him and tried to stop him but was slow from that old foot injury."

"He's broken enough hearts, don't let yours be one of them," Rose insisted. "Did he tell you your grandmother died of a broken heart? Bet he didn't."

"I heard brain aneurism."

"Yes, but we all knew very well he was breaking her heart. He knew it too. My paintings, my paintings. Always it was about him and the paintings. So where are those old coins now?"

There was a knock at the door and Rose routinely opened it to sign for packages. She shut the door and tossed the packages on the pile with all the others.

"Son-of-a-bitches keep sending junk. I don't want more things. I want cash."

"What's going on here, Rose? Why is this stuff piling up? There's rot in there. Is this some kind of cry for help? Do I have to call the men in white coats to come and haul you away?"

"Forget it, Concepción. The painting isn't here. I hocked it a couple days ago."

"The name is Tulsa. Is this some kind of addiction thing? Where's the money?"

"Gambled it."

"Tell me one thing, Rose, when you came back that night and sang to me, did you only come for the painting?

"What are you talking about? And, since when is your name Tulsa?"

"That night you left me at Pops. Do you remember you sang a lullaby? It was, you are my sunshine."

Rose sang while throwing away her empty beer bottle and retrieving another. "You are my sunshine, my only sunshine. You make me happy when skies are grey. You'll never know, dear, how much I love you. Please don't take my sunshine away," she finished and sits down. "I remember. I was carrying out the painting and saw you were watching me. So I sang until you were asleep again. I never stopped thinking about you and when I left, I honestly thought I was going to be right back, that I was getting our family together. I was a kid. Look, whatever pain Pops' silence might have caused you was no doubt far less than staying together."

"How nice for you that you have it all so neatly tied up in tidy little rationales."

Rose toasted toward me with her bottle of beer and drank it down.

I made some excuse, not even a believable one, to leave and pick up again in the morning.

Even though Rose is so transparently off-kilter, she had confidence and carried herself like the celebrity of her own life. She wasn't distant. Not like me, the life tourist. I guess everybody is entitled to tie pretty bows on the hard parts. After all, we are brought up that way. Aren't we? In our more ghastly moments as children, when the gaping maw of our room at night is just about to swallow us whole, in comes mother with a lullaby. Lullabies are pure trickery.

Apparently Lance was right there when I came out of Rose's room. He had ducked around a corner and watched me go to the Mustang and into the back seat. He watched me brush my teeth there in the parking lot using bottled water then headed to the room he had checked into earlier.

I took the pistol out and kept it with me while I slept under my blanket in the back seat of the Mustang.

Lance turned out the light and put his head down on the pillow. He closed his eyes but was soon at the window to check on me. He couldn't see the car well enough so he put on a jacket and went out. He peeked inside the car at me asleep in the back seat. He checked all the doors to make sure they were locked. He looked in at me again and saw that I had a gun in my hand. That relaxed him enough to go back to bed and fall asleep.

Rose sat up in bed drinking beer and crying.

The next morning, as I was about to knock on Rose's doo, Lance bounded up and startled me. He had three coffees and a bag of pastries.

"Your approach could use some polish. Here," he said, handing me the coffee.

"Didn't take you long to find me."

"Turns out your Grandfather's executor—"

"Blanche?"

"Blanche, yes. Turns out Blanche is not concerned about who she talks to or what information she gives out. Good to know, right? You're welcome."

Lance knocked. Rose opened the door and, seeing Lance, escorted him in, almost letting the door close in my face.

"Rose, this is my stalker, Lance. Lance, my estranged mother, Rose."

I had to rush past her into the bathroom and barely made it to vomit into the toilet. The bathroom door was wide open and I glanced at Rose who was at the front door signing for a stack of packages. She tossed them on the bed.

I reached up and flushed the toilet. Rose searched for a cloth for me which she soaked and put across my forehead. She gestured for Lance to help me to the bed. Rose was beside herself with worry about the time and the smell. She sprayed room deodorizer until she had us choking and we had to open the door and windows. Then she was in the bathroom leaning toward the mirror to put on her makeup.

"What'd you have for dinner?" Rose asked me.

"Canned sausages every day this week."

Rose looked to Lance for an explanation. He shrugged his shoulders. "Don't look at me. I'm not her dietitian. I'm her victim. She abandoned me and stole my car."

"Bought with my rent money."

"Hey, uh, Lance, do you like karaoke?"

"Love it, let's go."

Rose giggled and leaned closer to the mirror in the bathroom and carefully applied liquid liner.

The bar was in some kind of concrete bunker. The walls were unfinished and the room was murky and garishly lit in red and black lights. Lounging couches lined the raw concrete walls. A smattering of couples spoke in hushed tones. Why the Dollar? I wondered. They should change the name to the Mausoleum. I hope they know CPR here. This place is so boring some hearts are liable to slow to stopping. I chuckled, attracting a few glances. I smiled at them and shrugged. I should ask the DJ if he's got Mozart's *Requiem*. I laughed out loud attracting even more glances and a few stares. Smiled again and shrugged.

"Time to talk about the photos, Tulsa. Where are they?" Lance asked as he sat down near me with a couple beers.

Rose started in on the karaoke with a rhythm and blues classic directed at Lance. He enjoyed it and flirted back.

"I'm keeping the Mustang," I told him.

"I don't care, just give me the negatives and all prints."

"You have to sign the papers."

"Fine."

"Tulsa!" Rose said, walking up. She pulled up a chair and sat down.

I smiled at her. She smiled back distantly, distracted by a search for the waiter.

"I want to order a drink."

Lance stood. "I'll take care of it."

"Double Chivas on the rocks."

"I don't suppose you'll tell me where the painting is?" I asked her once Lance left.

Rose didn't respond. I took out my wallet and pulled out a hundred and set it down in front of her. I kept putting bills down without any response until finally Lance returned with drinks and put his hand on mine to stop me from going over one thousand dollars.

"Rose?"

She gathered the bills together and slapped my shoulder with the stack. "What's all this for, huh?" she asked with a dash of bitter.

"Rose?" Lance urged her, "That's your finder's fee."

She studied us with obvious suspicion then folded the bills and put them in her bra. "Fine by me," she chirped. "Pete's Pawn, right out here on the highway."

It wasn't easy but we made our way through the rubble to speak to Pete himself who was in back drinking from a gallon jug of cheap table wine and eating a hard-boiled egg.

"We came for the nude," I said.

He put down the egg and wine and stepped around the desk. "Yes, well, I do have a lot of original art here. A few are obviously schooled. I would recommend those. The others are what you might call outsider art."

"This would be a nude brought in recently, only days ago?" Lance added.

"Hold on," he said, going to the back of the shop. He returned with some paintings and displayed them here and there. Pops' painting wasn't among them.

"What's this?" I asked, irritated.

"That particular painting isn't here but there are some very interesting choices.

"Where is it?"

"Sold to a private buyer," Pete finally revealed.

"That painting was stolen and I have the paperwork to prove it. Should I call the police or can we call the buyer?"

"Of course, of course! I never knowingly deal in stolen items. I have a long standing reputation. Show me the papers and I will contact him."

"I'm sorry," Pete told us after going over the papers and talking to the buyer, "He refuses. He wants you to contact his lawyer."

"What? No! You tell him to get down here with that painting right now! You had no right to sell them in the first place. She only hocked them a couple days ago."

"Hocked them? Is that what she told you?"

"This is a pawn shop."

"Right but I also sell to collectors."

"Excuse us a moment?" Lance asked Pete then pulled me aside out of ear shot and showed me a business card. "While you were chatting with Pete, I was looking around his desk. It's all there by the phone, receipts, everything. Let's go. I have an idea. I help you recover the painting and you give me the negatives and prints. Deal?"

"Deal."

I waited in the car for Lance to retrieve his pack from his room at the motel. I looked at Rose's door and hoped a delivery guy would come and I could watch her one last time while she signed for a package.

Lance returned wearing all black.

"Who died?"

Lance tossed his pack in the back seat and got in. I glanced at Rose's door one last time before heading back out, probably never seeing her again. My stomach tightened as I drove down the boulevard away from the motel.

"Pull over here," Lance said.

I pulled over and watched him go into a little party shop. I looked at my reflection and applied lipstick. Checked for lipstick on my teeth. Lance got in and put a shopping bag from the party store on the back seat and gave me a bottle of water.

"What's that about?"

"You ready to go? I am."

"Are you going to tell me where?"

"Go up to the next light and turn onto the highway."

During the drive Lance told stories about his childhood. How seldom he saw his parents and how much they were like strangers. It was always formal with them. At first his stories were anecdotal and entertaining. Then he went deeper and it became very personal. Suddenly everything was serious and I was terrified to say anything because I didn't want to say the wrong thing, not while he was baring his soul. It was annoying.

Lance leaving the family and slumming wasn't anything new. He was off slumming at sixteen. He would go out to a party and not be seen for days, sometimes weeks. They never had to call the police because he had a driver with him everywhere and that guy would always call. The driver was only ten years older than Lance but had enough life experience to be a lot wiser. The family came to rely on him and he and Lance grew up together in a lot of ways.

"The reason I'm telling you all this about Marco is so you will understand the magnitude of what he did for me," Lance explained.

Lance hadn't just been slumming, he was down in it and started spending a lot of time around addicts and criminals. To Lance it was all fascinating and like a trip to another country. He didn't have to live like the people he was visiting and he would never know their suffering. His children will never know and neither will their children. This safe distance made Lance reckless and Marco's job more difficult.

Something happened which neither Marco nor Lance are willing to divulge. The crux of it was that Lance got into trouble with the law and Marco incriminated himself somehow so he would be able to accompany Lance who ended up doing time. Obviously Lance and his family owed Marco big time. It was Lance's idiocy that got them both locked up.

"Okay, exit here."

Lance directed me to a lovely older neighborhood in a hilly area overlooking the town. He had me park in a cul-de-sac.

"Okay, wait here. I will be right back," Lance told me and handed me a piece of paper with Marco's phone number on it.

"Call Marco if anything happens and of course it won't." He took something out of the party bag and put it in his pack.

"Wait, where are we?" I asked, looking around.

Lance put the pack on his back then disappeared into some shrubbery. I looked around again. There were too many tall old trees to tell anything about where we were.

All those trees blocked out the sun and it was dark there in the cul-de-sac. I took the pistol out from under the seat and ran through the shrubbery after Lance. When I caught up to him he was approaching the back of a house. I touched his shoulder and he spun around ready to fight. He was wearing a children's dog mask too small for his face which made me laugh. He took a kids' cat mask out and made me put it on.

"I can't help feel we're losing the upper hand here, Lance." I held the Colt .45 up hoping to intimidate with the size. Lance glanced back at me and stopped when he saw the pistol.

"Are you out of your mind? What is that? That belongs in a museum!"

The outdoor motion sensor lights went on and dogs started barking.

"Oh great now we are going to prison because you can't tell the difference between antiquity and utility!"

"You know what's antiquated, your thuggish solutions to life's problems. Something amiss? Oh, I'll just brute my way through."

The buyer came around the corner in his robe, holding a .38 which made me smile and hold my bigger gun a little higher. We looked ridiculous so the owner was obviously not very threatened by us.

"Mind telling me why you are having a spat on my property, dressed like that?"

Lance removed his mask and mine.

"What is going on? Is that a real gun?"

"Colt .45 Six Shooter, actually," I corrected.

He held his hand out for it and I was reluctant to hand it over. Lance took it out of my hand and gave it to the buyer. The buyer was obviously very impressed with it.

"That's a family heirloom. It has papers and everything so its value and traceability are one and the same. Interesting tidbit."

"I can explain, Lance offered. "We came for the nude painting. It is the original work of her grandfather who was just killed."

"Come with me," He said, directing us by gunpoint to the front of the house.

"How much did you pay for it?" I asked the buyer.

"Not now," Lance said to me.

"Not much," the buyer said.

"I'll give you a thousand for it. Give it to him, Lance."

Lance checked his wallet.

"Will you take seven? It's all I have on me."

"And I'll take that pistol back," I added.

The Buyer lowered his gun and took the money. He made sure my pistol wasn't loaded before returning it to me.

"Are you really the artist's granddaughter?"

"Yes, I am."

"Do you have anything else of his you can leave with me?"

"I can let you know when there is a show."

"I would like that. Wait here," the owner said then went into the house. He returned with the painting and Lance took it. The owner gave me his business card.

"You won't forget?"

"I promise," I reassured him.

When Lance loaded the painting in the trunk he made a point of having a look at it.

"Beautiful," he said, truly impressed by the work. "This is your grandmother?"

"I used to go into his studio when he wasn't home to look at how the paintings were turning out and compare them to the women who showed up to model for weeks at a time. This was something entirely different."

"He loved her, you can tell by looking at it," he said, closing the trunk.

"Have you ever been in love?" I asked Lance, once we were in the car.

"Never. Though there was that au pair. No, that wasn't love so, no. You?"

"Never. It seems like such an all or nothing proposition."

"It has to be. If a species isn't compelled to protect their young it could not survive. I'm still angry at my mother for taking off. Let's go, you can drop me off somewhere but let's go by my dad's place first. We can sneak in the back and pick up some of my clothes. Bring the film. Our deal, remember? I'll think of someplace you can drop me then I'll sign the car's papers over."

I looked at him skeptically. He incapacitated me with that blinding smile so I started the car and headed out.

19

Lance unlocked the gate at the back side of the walled-in grounds and we went in. It was thick with wildly growing trees, shrubbery, ferns, and grasses. Lance led me, scraped and cut–of course because I was wearing a cocktail dress and pumps–to the more manicured trail through well kept, arboreal grounds.

"Thank you so much," I said, brushing leaves and cobwebs off and picking stems from my hair. When I looked up and saw the chateau, I was struck by its size.

"Wow. You really are slumming."

Lance grabbed my wrist and pulled me off the trail through a cluster of trees and along a less visible back route to the cottage.

Though it was called a cottage, it was nothing like the three quarter structure we had lived in together–which I maintain was built in the thirties for little people on contract with one of the film studios. This cottage consisted of two stories, a few bedrooms and bathrooms upstairs, a few guest rooms, entertainment, and dining downstairs. We entered through the back door to the kitchen. Marco was in there preparing dinner.

"Please tell me there isn't a trail of broken laws behind you," he said, brandishing the chopping knife at Lance. They hugged like brothers. Marco looked at me and smiled. I suspected he sized me up quickly and surmised that Lance brought me in through the jungle out back.

"No matter how hard I tried. You remember that crazy situation over there at the Madam's house? Here's the residual consequence."

"Madam?" I asked.

"Tulsa, this is Marco the indispensable. Thus the free crash pad, which only proves, yet again, that my father loves him more than me."

"Hi Tulsa," Marco said, extending his hand. "You can see why that's true if you spend any time with him. Or me."

"Clearly he enjoys a more rectal habitat," I contributed.

Both Marco and Lance's eyebrows shot up. Marco put his arm around my shoulders and escorted me into the main room of the cottage.

"Grab the beers," Marco told Lance over his shoulder. Lance retrieved a few bottles of wine and glasses.

The ceiling was very high. On one side of the room were a billiard table and other entertainments. On the other was a lounge area. There were a lot of potted grasses, palms, and trees.

"So you know each other from jail?"

"Long before that," Lance reminded me.

"Oh yeah. What was it? Larceny?"

"Knows you pretty well, bro," Marco commented.

"Is the Mustang stolen?" I asked Lance.

"Nope. That's bought free and clear," Lance told us.

"Right, probably with my rent money," I told Marco. He chuckled.

"Marco here is head of security for my father. Tulsa took pictures of me with the Madam and some others in the red room without our knowledge."

"What? What others? What are you talking about?" I said, thrown off a bit.

"Is that right? Sounds compromising. Why did she do that?" Marco asked, looking at me. "Is there some reason you would want compromising pictures of them?"

I stepped away. "What? No! Why? Are you suggesting I should?"

Lance slumped in exasperated impatience.

"I'm clueless. What do we do with her?"

"It's in my pack, right here." I took the film out of my pack and tossed it over to Lance.

"Did you know I played pro football?" Marco asked me.

"He likes to remind me of his physical dominance over me. But what he forgets is that he is essentially the help," Lance explained.

"He enjoys lording over me. I am told he has better breeding but as you pointed out, he could use some manners," Marco added.

They wrestled at first playfully then started to hurt each other.

"Okay, I'm off to see the wizard. Nice meeting you, Marco."

Lance, a bit beaten and bloody, grabbed me by the arm and sat me down.

"I don't think so, Dorothy. Have a seat."

"At least eat before you go, I was just about to cook something," Marco offered.

"I'm starving. Damn it. Okay. But I'm out of here directly after. You guys are creeping me out."

Lance and Marco chuckled.

I had not eaten in a very long time and I couldn't seem to get enough food. I was unaware of the two of them watching me and exchanging glances. Lance poured more wine. I had yet to take a sip of mine.

"So here's what I was thinking, Marco, we both try to impregnate her that way we double the chance of it working. Tell father it's mine no matter whose it is then he has to bring me back in."

I chuckled but then looked up at Lance and thought maybe he was serious.

"Too late, I'm already pregnant."

"What did I tell you, I knew it," Lance said to Marco.

"I wasn't going to tell you because I don't want anything to do with you. So you can forget your gang rape plans," I said, standing.

Marco chuckled again.

"I'm leaving now. I'm going out that door. Don't you dare stop me or come after me. I will get my name on the Mustang's papers by claiming you abandoned it so you better back me up, Lance."

I grabbed my pack and went out the front of the cottage. Lance called after me "Follow the same trail back."

Marco stepped in front of me. "Let me take you. Make sure you get to your car safely," he suggested, setting his hand on my shoulder.

"Take your hand off of me," I said then left.

As soon as I went out that door I realized I didn't have anywhere to go. At some point I had to make sure the paintings were properly stored and settle up all the legal business but in the meantime I had no idea where I was going to rest my head. I was so tired I could lie down and sleep right there. It wasn't long before I was lost and shortly ended up next to the main house. There was a light on in a basement room with windows so I went over and looked inside.

In what looked like a library or reading room was a gentleman in a chair smoking a cigar and reading *The 120 Days of Sodom*, by the Marquis de Sade and chuckling here and there.

A light blasted on me from a flashlight and a security guard held me at gun point and demanded my pack. I gave it to him and raised my hands. A second security guard came up and patted me down while the first guard went through my pack. He found the Colt and showed it to his partner.

"Let's go," the first one said to me.

I was led at gunpoint around the front of the house to the foyer where they sat me down and one watched me while the other used the house phone.

"Marco? …Yes we did. Outside the library. …Yes, she's here in the foyer."

I stood up and started walking toward Marco when he came in but my guard stepped in front of me. Marco went to the phone to make a call.

"Yes it is her. …Pregnant. …Lance. …We believe so. …It wasn't loaded, no sir. …I agree. Best for everyone. …Thank you, sir."

Marco hung up and had a quiet conversation with the guard who had taken my pack. Marco took the pistol and pack over to me.

"Go ahead and check the contents to make sure everything is there." Marco instructed, holding the pack open.

I looked in it for the coins and felt the weight of the monadero. I nodded and he took the pack away.

"Okay, it's all set. You will sleep here tonight, have a good breakfast and then be on your way."

"What do you mean all set? I don't remember being in on that conversation. Can I have my stuff now?" I asked pointing at my pack.

"You will be escorted to your room and I will see you at breakfast. Afterward, I will take you to the car and return your firearm and the rest. Good night, Tulsa."

"Wait, Marco, hold on. Am I a guest or a prisoner? And, by the way, I have valuables in there."

"I will keep it in the safe overnight."

Marco gestured for the guard to leave. A maid came down the stairs and before I could say another word, Marco left and I was alone with her.

The maid led me through a few rooms on the main floor. I was so tired I focused solely on her and the bed promised wherever we were going. Then we passed an entry that caught my attention and I went back to look inside. Water from a pool reflected against the wall of the entry. I went in, followed by the maid.

"The grotto."

On one side was a wall of glass panes and steel that ran along the building and curved at the top to become part of the ceiling. The room was filled with palms, ferns, rubber and other trees, ground coverings, moss, and grasses. The air was fresh and sweet. The grotto arched over half the pool and along the back of the shallow cavern visible inside was a stone bench and colored lights.

"Shall we see if you have permission to bathe here?"

I nodded. The maid went to the house phone near the pool to check. I looked up at the starry blue sky visible above the glass-paned ceiling.

After verifying it was "permitted," I removed my clothes and slowly walked down a short ramp into the pool and swam into the grotto. I sat at the back, on the stone bench, partially in the water. The maid waited at the edge with a towel and robe. I went under the water and swam from the deep to the shallow end.

I was suddenly aware of being cradled in my great-grandmother's arm. She sang a lullaby to me while she lay dying.

Again, suddenly I was sitting on the branch of a walnut tree next to a naked infant girl. Crows were quietly perched around us.

"I figured as much. I'm pregnant, aren't I?" I asked. Only then did I realize that she didn't have an indent above her lip yet.

"I'm sorry," she said.

"What? Why?"

"I have to go."

"What? Why do you have to go? Don't go."

"It sometimes happens this way."

"Why? It doesn't have to. Stay here with me. You don't have to go."

"We must always be ready to say our good-byes. Such is the way of life. As we leave we also meet and both are just as sweet."

"Abuela?"

The crows flew away leaving me alone in the barren walnut tree.

—⚡—

I opened my eyes and looked at the ceiling.

"Welcome back," said the doctor standing next to my bed in the hospital room, listening to my heart.

—m—

I had been dressed and ready to go for twenty minutes but wanted to finish the end of the movie I had been watching on TV. It was that old western, *Shane*. I sat on the edge of the bed alone in the room, watching TV. A nurse came along and poked her head in.

"Somebody coming for you?"

"Nope, riding solo."

The nurse stepped in and watched the movie with me for a minute.

"He did what he had to do, Joey. You don't hate Shane," Jean Arthur explained.

"I know, mother. Shane?" Joey calls out but Shane is by then too far to hear.

"Joey can't bear that the last thing he said to Shane was that he hated him. He knows he will never see him again. Shane is a nomad. Like me and my dad."

"Just riding through?" the nurse asked.

"Wait, not like me. Just my dad. I'm done that," I clarified.

The nurse nodded her approval and I walked out.

The Mustang was parked right out front. I went through the doors and looked around the front of the hospital for Lance. Marco wheeled up a chair to roll me the last few feet to the car.

"I'm very sorry to hear about your baby, Tulsa."

"Where's Lance?"

"I wish I knew how to explain the way things are with this family. Lance was not told where you were taken and is forbidden to see you."

"Right, and you won't tell him or he never asked. Either way, I don't care. I'm done with you both." I tried to walk around him but he blocked me.

"Okay, I'll drive you wherever you need to go and leave the car with you. I just have to report back that I left you somewhere safely."

Marco handed my pack over to me.

"Lance wanted me to make sure to look after this for you. He said you never let it out of your sight. Must be all that gold. Which is still there, safe and sound."

I checked to make sure the gold and pistol were there.

"It has been in my personal possession since that night. I was the one who pulled you out and resuscitated you.

"Keys," I said, holding out my hand.

Marco dropped the keys into my palm.

I tossed the pack into the car. He smiled and I got in and drove away.

20

I sat at my desk typing away at a new typewriter. Next to the typewriter, the old stack of papers, stained, disheveled, and wrinkled. On the other side were freshly typed pages. After the last sentence, I sat back for a moment. Then I typed "E N D," and pulled that last page out to add to the stack.

It had all now finally gone from me and in going left me to myself.

I straightened the pages and slid the stack into an envelope. I wrote Rose's name and address on the outside, put stamps on it, and took it with me out of the apartment.

I put the envelope in a mailbox in front of the used book store. I unlocked and pushed aside the gate then unlocked and opened the front door. I flipped around the open sign and switched on the lights. On the way to the register I checked my mail. Behind the register, on the wall, was a framed dollar bill. Next to that was the framed Polaroid of me with Rose and Pops. Next to that was a shadow box containing the photo of Concepción in her quinceañera dress with the heirloom Colt .45 and empty monadero.

Weeks later, Rose came in to the store. Spotting me, she came up and tossed the pages toward me. They scattered over the floor between us.

"What the hell is that?"

I was so happy to see her, I walked over the carpet of scattered typed pages to hug her. At first Rose's arms remained at her side but I hugged her tighter. Rose's arms came up and she hugged me back.

21

Cars lined the downtown street. People spilled out of the gallery to chat or smoke along the sidewalk. A bus pulled over at the stop across the street and Blanche came out. She jaywalked across to the entrance and went inside. Rose came down the street on the arm of a drunken cowboy and they went into the gallery.

Inside, toward the back of the exhibit of Pops' work, Blanche studied the painting of herself at 40 years-old that had been as restored as possible after I had cut it. The buyer that Lance and I tried robbing was standing next to Blanche admiring the same painting. He glanced at Blanche and when he realized she was the woman in the painting, he smiled flirtatiously at her. She bestowed her bright Maraschino smile on him.

Rose looked at the painting with herself nursing in Concepción's arms. It was the centerpiece of the exhibit. She fixated on the sweetness of the child, of herself when she was a child.

I studied *The Birthday Series* which was exhibited with the original photos. Pops painted me gazing right at him with an open, beautiful smile in each painting. It occurred to me only then that he had wanted me happy but was too handicapped by intense self-engagement to actually make me happy. Isn't that something? And that is how you want someone's happiness and break their heart at the same time. It seemed to me that when he titled the paintings *The Birthday Series* he was referring to himself. His heart had awakened and he bestowed the only happiness he knew he ever could, painting those and willing them to me.

"Here's to you, Pops," I said, raising my glass and toasting.

Lance and Marco made their way over and I greeted them with hugs. They made fun of my expressions in the photos Pops took when I was imagining terrible fates on him. Malevolence makes ugly. Lance and Marco cajoled me and made faces to mock my expressions until they had me laughing at myself with them.

I realized then that I harbored no ill will or resentment toward any of them. My heart was finally truly free.

About The Author

Michelle Espinosa grew up in Los Angeles, South Dakota, and lived in Mexico, resulting in her distinctive voice as writer/filmmaker. Her work has been described as disturbing and dream-like. The New York Times described her award winning short film, *Pinfeathers*, as having a "Salammbô-like decadence." *Pinfeathers* received a Silver Plaque at the Chicago International Film Festival.

Michelle is a team coordinator for Alternatives to Violence Project for three days each month at a local prison. She is also a volunteer member of the Los Angeles Mayor's Crisis Response Team who are called on scene after a fatality to assist witnesses and family members. By request, she developed *Communication and Conflict Resolution in a Crisis* training for the team to strengthen their communication and conflict resolution skills on-scene. She trains community members in conflict resolution and, as a mediator/facilitator for seventeen years with the Los Angeles City Attorney's office, she also trains and coaches adult mediators as well as peer mediators in L.A. schools.

Made in the USA
Charleston, SC
20 December 2014